EMBRACE THE NIGHT

EMBRACE THE NIGHT

Caris Roane

Formatting and cover by Bella Media Management.

ISBN-13: 978-1511961516

THE BLOOD ROSE SERIES
BOOK FIVE

EMBRACE THE NIGHT

CARIS ROANE

Dear Reader,

Welcome to the fifth installment of the Blood Rose Series, **EMBRACE THE NIGHT**. In this book, Mastyr Jude hungers for the Port Townsend bar owner, Hannah. But how can he make a move on a woman that he gave piggy-back rides to when she was a little girl? That Hannah seems willing, doesn't help things at all!

He's ignored his deepest needs for a hundred years…

Mastyr Vampire Jude has kept his distance from all women because he lost his wife and daughter to an enemy attack a hundred years ago. He won't go through that kind of loss again. And he won't jeopardize another woman's life while the deadly Invictus wraith-pairs still pose a threat in the Nine Realms. But when Hannah saves his life by creating unexpected fire from the palms of her hands, he knows that something 'very realm' is going on with her and he can no longer ignore his long-suppressed desire for the beautiful owner of the Gold Rush bar. When his cravings for her blood and her body drive him to take her to bed and tap into her vein, his world shifts forever. But can Hannah make the adjustment to a life lived on the frontlines of an ongoing war? And if anything should happen to her, how could he ever live with himself?

Enjoy!

Caris Roane

For the latest releases, hottest pics, and coolest contests, be sure to sign up for my newsletter!!!

http://www.carisroane.com/contact-2/

Book #6, Malik and Willow's story: EMBRACE THE WILD!!!

Now available: http://www.carisroane.com/6-embrace-the-wild/

Be sure to check out the Blood Rose Tales – TRAPPED, HUNGER, and SEDUCED -- shorter works for a quick, sexy, satisfying read. For more information: http://www.carisroane.com/blood-rose-tales-box-set/

Chapter One

Hannah Osborne had become a stupid cliché: Hot man, cold shower.

She refused to turn away from the communications monitor, even though Mastyr Jude had just arrived and now stood behind her in the doorway. All his gorgeousness had become a lot to manage in recent weeks and she was working hard to restrain her waywardness where the powerful Mastyr of Kellcasse was concerned.

She'd asked Jude to set up the new communication center inside her bar, the Gold Rush, since so many of his kind spent hours at her establishment.

Jude had always come to the Gold Rush, but his visits had increased by *a lot* over the past few months. She wanted to tell him not to come around so much because she currently lusted after the man. Amazingly, the words would never leave her throat.

"So, what's the latest on the loop?" His deep voice sent shivers down her spine.

Hannah belonged to a small, select email loop that included only women. All the women who worked the U.S. access city centers were on the loop as well as the four women currently bonded to mastyrs of the Nine Realms. Hannah had learned so much about the blood rose phenomenon that was sweeping through each realm that she often wondered when Jude's blood rose would show up.

But each time she had that thought, for some reason her fingers would curl until she made tight little fists with both hands and her jaw clenched. She wanted the best for Jude, of course, but another woman climbing all over him made her skin grow hot in the worst way.

Even now, she had to take a moment to calm herself. So, yeah, in the past few months, she'd kind of gotten out of control where the Kellcasse mastyr was concerned.

"Hannah, are you ignoring me?"

"No … that is, what was your question?"

"What's the word on the loop?"

Oh, that. "Everyone's talking about what happened in Kellcasse, on North Island."

"You mean the massacre."

"Yes." Hannah hadn't wanted to use that word because it made it horribly real. Two families of trolls had been slaughtered by the Invictus, which in itself wasn't unusual, unfortunately. But what remained a mystery was that it appeared not one member of either family tried to hide, run away, or even fight back. All realm-folk fought when the terrifying wraith-pairs attacked. "Has your forensics team come up with anything yet?"

He shook his head. "We still don't have a clear answer about what happened out there. Invictus got to them, of course, but no one knows why there were no signs of defensive wounds. And trolls always have places to hide."

The lack of an answer made Hannah's skin crawl, though she didn't know why. Her palms started tingling as well, something that had been happening a lot lately. She rubbed them together, trying to get rid of the sensation. Probably just nerves. "I really hope one day you'll be able to bring the ancient fae down and end the Invictus threat once and for all."

"With everything I hold sacred, I do, too."

She almost turned to look at Jude because he'd spoken his heart. But she forced herself to remain fixed on her Internet tabs, moving between her email account and her favorite realm-based email loop, then back. She kept typing a response to the Tennessee communications center, fearing if she turned to face Jude she'd get lost all over again.

Jude only had to show up at her bar and her whole body heated up like she had a fever. And for reasons she believed had mostly to do with the sheer breadth of his massive shoulders, her overall rise in body temperature wouldn't dissipate until the damn man left her sight.

She'd even resorted to using the bunkroom shower and a lot of cold water to cool down. And that water was *cold!* Again, so cliché.

She'd installed the large bunkroom a few years ago to house overnight, sun-sensitive realm-folk. Sometimes, members of Jude's Vampire Guard would come in for a pint at the end of a long night battling and stay for a few more rounds. As soon as the sun showed the first rays of its blistering heat, they headed to the bunkroom and at certain times of the year this far north that hour came early.

But Hannah was happy to offer shelter to any of them, especially the Guardsmen, because they laid down their lives every night for their fellow realm-folk.

"Are you ever going to turn around and talk to me? Or are you just going to keep typing?"

The smart thing would be to keep typing. "Hold on. I'm almost done."

"I think you're avoiding me."

Duh.

And more heat because that voice of his, dipping into the lowest timbres, slid all the way down her chest and abdomen, making her feel things she really shouldn't. Perspiration popped on her forehead.

She'd known Jude since she was a child, so it seemed strange to have *feelings* for someone who had given her piggy-back rides.

She paused in her typing to massage her hands once more. They were tingling again, which also happened anytime Jude showed up. Tingling hands, flushed skin, sweating. Even her heart felt laden when he was near.

She had it bad.

If every once in a while she suspected something more realm-ish might be at work with her fairly recent interest in the Mastyr of Kellcasse, she ignored the thought. She was one-hundred-percent human and had no interest in hooking-up with a vampire.

So, she kcpt typing.

Despite her love of realm-folk generally, and that the Gold Rush had been a gathering place for their kind for three decades, she'd never seen herself as having any kind of future away from Port Townsend. She loved her bar, her cliff-side home, her Puget Sound lifestyle. She'd never even dated a realm man, just humans, which was another reason that her sudden profound lust for Jude had come as such a surprise.

The whole thing had started about four months ago. She'd been re-stocking cleaning supplies when he'd come into the small space. She'd intended to greet him, maybe even give him a hug which she offered to all the Guardsmen for the hard work they performed every night of their lives.

But as she turned and met his smoky gray eyes, some kind of switch got thrown deep inside her feminine soul. He'd been almost family to her and just like that, she wanted to see his broad shoulders without his shirt on. Even her nipples had puckered with sudden profound interest, something he'd noticed because she'd been wearing a t-shirt. Hard to disguise aroused nipples through a silk bra and a thin layer of cotton.

He hadn't said anything for a long moment, just stared at her breasts. He'd blinked a couple of times, and the closet, barely big enough for both of them, soon filled with a very peppery-spicy, masculine scent that clipped her at the back of her knees.

She tottered and would have fallen, but he caught her arm and held her up. "You okay, Hannah?"

He'd searched her eyes, and she nodded but very slowly like she was moving underwater.

She'd made up some excuse about not having eaten all day, but ever since that closet incident, she'd been lit up like a Neon sign, despite the fact that she ignored him as much as she could.

Of course it was hard to pretend Jude didn't exist in a room about twelve-feet square since Jude was built like a tank. Muscles on muscles.

His deep voice, resonating with a number of delicious layers, rolled over her. "So how are you, Hannah?"

Just keep typing.

Her breathing faltered. “I’m fine. Heard you came in earlier with a couple of your Guardsmen just to wrap up the night.”

“I did, but I sent them off a bit ago. Wanted to have a word with you before I left. I’ve got about twenty minutes to get my ass back to my house in central Kellcasse.”

“You can always stay in the bunkroom.” She kept her fingers moving, but her cheeks flamed. Would he misinterpret the suggestion as a come-on?

“I know, but I’m a fast flyer. I’ll make it.”

Jude was a fast everything, the most powerful vampire in his realm.

“What’s up?” Just trying to keep things friendly and even.

“I haven’t seen you in a few days. Everything okay in here?”

“The center is humming, as usual. Your techs did a brilliant job setting everything up. But you know that.” Clack, clack, clack.

The communications room was a recent addition to the back of her bar, part of a Nine Realms plan to keep messages flowing outside the realms. The enemy, known as Margetta the ancient fae, had ways of blocking realm-to-realm communications. Centers in access point cities, like Port Townsend, kept information moving swift and sure among all nine mastyr vampires.

This time, Jude drew close and once more she struggled to breathe, his peppery scent hitting her hard. He smelled like something you’d rub on meat and cook for a long time. Allspice maybe.

She took a slow drag through both nostrils, and her body heated up a little more.

He leaned close, ostensibly to look at the monitor, but she knew he struggled as she did, feeling things he didn’t want to feel either. She often caught him staring at her with a hungry look, or checking her out when she moved through a room.

She'd been no different.

"So you've been emailing back and forth with Lebanon."

"Yes, they wanted to know about North Island, and of course I've had little info. But I just updated them with what you told me."

"I'm liking all the back and forth."

"Me, too. I mean, it makes total sense." Why did he have to smell so good?

"You are ignoring me."

At that, Hannah clicked 'send', then swiveled in her chair to face him. He was so close though, that she had to push her chair sideways or they would have collided. "No, I haven't. Really. Why would you say that?"

Those eyes.

His gray eyes, surrounded as they were with thick lashes, always hit her stomach like a hard punch these days. He had thick, straight brows that made him look ferocious when he frowned. His nose had a slight hawkish appearance and his cheekbones looked sculpted. But it was his thick, curly, black hair that made him look wild, dangerous and unbelievably handsome. How many times had she thought about removing his Guardsman clasp so that she could spend a half hour or so getting her fingers all tangled up.

He was a man's man at a muscular six-five. Built on massive lines, he was eye-candy of the most savory. Several of her girlfriends had ordered her to call them the moment he showed up at the Gold Rush. They'd arrive ten minutes later, a flock of seagulls descending on a seashore feast.

Did he want two kids? Three? Maybe a dozen?

He flashed a set of brilliant white teeth and her stomach squeezed up. One smile and he could bring down an entire room full of women.

His voice once more filled the room. "Why do I think you were ignoring me? Because you kept typing when you knew I was standing in the doorway. Or do I just annoy you like a cranky forest gremlin these days? Or maybe I bore you."

She couldn't help but chuckle. She'd never seen a forest gremlin, but she'd heard plenty of stories so she could imagine what he meant. "You could never bore me. Your life is too interesting and way too dangerous to be boring. So what would you like to know? Although, I'm sure your Kellcasse center has kept you informed?"

He smiled. "Yes, and you were right to recommend Longeness for the job. He's detail-oriented and keeps everything moving. So, thank you for that."

"Well, you're welcome. I just had a feeling he'd work out for you." Jude had built a communication center in Kellcasse about the same time he'd set up this center in her bar. She'd known Longeness and his wife, both fae, for years since they'd made her bar a second home on their date-nights.

Jude glanced around. The room didn't have windows, one of the requirements for the access point centers, that way a vampire or a fae would never have to worry about light-and-sun issues. "I wanted to give you a heads up as well. We had a rough encounter about an hour ago. Really strange, though, because we chased a wraith-pair out over the Sound, if you can believe that."

"You're kidding." Hannah was surprised. The deadly wraith-pairs rarely if ever crossed the access point lines. "What were they doing out here?"

Jude shrugged. "Hell if I know." But something in his expression concerned Hannah.

He eased back against the long, steel-reinforced counter, crossing his arms over his chest. At least he'd left his way-too-sexy Guardsman coat in the bar area of the building, but still looked amazing in his loose woven, maroon shirt, snug battle leathers, and hip boots that had several small intricate silver medallions running up and down the side seams. Lately she'd felt an impulse to touch the medallions, one more sign she was out-of-control when it came to the man.

Jude shifted his gaze away from her and frowned. He dragged air through his nostrils and his jaw ground a couple of times. She knew something was troubling him; he'd been uneasy since he'd helped Mastyr Seth battle the ancient fae a few months ago.

She admired the hell out of Jude. He cared about his men and took his duties as mastyr of his realm seriously. No one loved the beautiful, forested island realm of Kellcasse more than Jude. And he saved lives every night of his life by battling wraith-pairs.

She reached out and clasped him on the shoulder. "What's going on?"

He met her gaze and grimaced, but nodded.

His smile reappeared as he turned to look at her. "You want me to spill my guts?"

She tilted her head. She wouldn't stand for bullshit, not from him or anyone. "Yes, I want to know why, for a moment there, you looked like the world was about to crash down on your head."

~ ~ ~

Jude stared into eyes the color of a beautiful sunset, the kind when the sky goes all violet just before it drifts to gray. No one had eyes like Hannah Osborne, not even some of the more exotic fae in his Realm. She ran the Port Townsend Realm Communication Center that connected every earth access point city with all the other cities. Hannah basically managed this center and kept it working like a well-oiled machine with several employees rotating shifts during the day and night. Some were Realm, others were humans who enjoyed the company of realm-folk, the latter quality one of Hannah's prerequisites for the job when she did the interviewing.

So, yeah, the center hummed.

She was tall, almost six feet, and he liked that about her. Though she was very fair and almost delicate in her features, she had a strength about her that pleased him and which was the main reason he'd agreed to let her be in charge of the center.

She wore her light brown hair loose about her shoulders. It had a slight curl and golden highlights. With arched brows, thick lashes and full lips, she was a damn beautiful woman.

He'd known her for years and could even remember a time when as a kid she sat on the bar, throwing darts at the dart board clear across the room. This misuse of the darts had brought her father in from the backroom, his face red with rage.

'You could hurt someone, girl.' He always called his daughter 'girl' when she was in trouble. Hannah had gotten in big trouble and because Jude had encouraged her to misbehave, he'd gone after her.

Finding her sitting on the back step and crying her eyes out, he'd slid an arm around her young, boney shoulders until she hiccupped through a couple of sobs and finally let go of her girlish pain. He'd then given her a piggy-back ride until she was laughing again.

He'd always liked her spirit.

He still did.

But he needed to keep thinking of Hannah like that, young and innocent. However, it was really hard when her shirt had just enough of a V-cut to reveal a line of cleavage he'd been lusting after for several months now.

The whole messed up situation had begun in that stupid supply closet. He'd gone there to ask her something about one of the access centers and had somehow gotten lost in her beautiful breasts that grew puckered then and there. And from that point, his cravings for Hannah had all but taken over.

He'd tried to keep his distance, but every time he promised himself to skip a visit to the Gold Rush, he'd head there anyway.

Something had erupted between them in that moment, something new, vital, and damn sexual.

And he absolutely loved the new perfume she'd taken to wearing. She smelled like roses and seashells, which didn't make a lot of sense, but she did, like if he walked through a rose garden right by the water's edge, that's what she would smell like. The trouble was, when he caught the scent of her perfume, his body lit up and he wanted nothing more than to pick her up in his arms and fly her to his home in Kellcasse. Maybe keep her there for a decade.

He'd had several 'moments' with her in recent weeks, when her gaze caught and held or she accidentally brushed up against him in the bar and he couldn't seem to catch his breath.

He also knew whatever was going on was mutual to the point that lately he'd started thinking about actually asking for a date. He held back, though. She was little Hannah, the one called 'girl', the human, for Goddess's sake.

And he wasn't into long-term anything. He'd made that decision a century ago when his wife and daughter had died. He didn't ever want to feel that kind pain again, not until the ancient fae was dead and the last of the Invictus burned on a funeral pyre.

But right now, she wanted him to talk about what was troubling him.

He debated the matter in his head for a full minute and to her credit, she let him be, let him live with his own thoughts and sort this one out.

Finally, he drew a deep breath and decided to open up. "I never talked much, to anyone, about what happened in Walvashorr with the shifter packs."

Her arched brows rose, but she made no comment, which once more encouraged him to continue. "I saw the ancient fae. She was surrounded by a strange powerful golden light, but she smelled evil, like something rotting behind a dumpster."

Hannah grunted softly. Glancing at her, he saw that she'd wrinkled her nose. "Was the imagery too strong?" he asked.

"If it was accurate, then you couldn't have said it better. We all know that smell."

"Yeah, we do." He nodded several times. "Mastyr Seth has a woman now, his blood rose, and I'm sure Lorelei has shared things on your loop." He waved a hand to encompass her computer monitor. "You know, the one with all you women."

"Yeah, all us women." She smiled. She had lovely teeth, white, perfectly straight, nicely shaped incisors. Shit, he even liked the woman's teeth.

He frowned at Hannah for a moment, searching those violet eyes again. She'd struck up a serious friendship with several of the women bonded to mastyr vampires and the email loop seemed to be blazing or at least simmering all the time.

He knew she'd switched tabs the moment he'd arrived on the threshold to the room. She'd done that before, protecting everyone's privacy, so he wasn't surprised. He'd once asked her about it, teasing her, but she'd lifted her chin. "What we women say in confidence, especially about you men, you don't need to know. It's a sacred, womanish thing."

'A womanish thing'. Another reminder that the child had grown up. And she really wasn't a child. She was twenty-eight, but against his two-hundred-years she was considerably younger in life-experience.

He forced his thoughts back to what it was he wanted to say to Hannah. "Here's the thing. Margetta planned this attack on Walvashorr Realm, really planned it. And when Seth and I went to rescue Lorelei, I saw the ancient fae's army encampment. The level of military organization astounded me because wraith-pairs, aren't by definitions, soldiers. They don't group together and form joint goals."

Hannah nodded. "Which means, Margetta has somehow taken charge of the wraith-pairs and can control them."

"She's being very deliberate and I'm worried for Kellcasse, and concerned that Margetta will come after us and we won't be ready. It's been months now and everything's been quiet in all the realms."

Even as he spoke the words aloud, he wasn't sure what was prompting him to share this with Hannah. But because of her association with the communications center and with the other powerful women bonded to a few of his fellow mastyrs, she knew a lot about the current war with Margetta. "The problem is, I don't know what kind of strategy she would devise against Kellcasse, what her goal would be. With Seth's Realm, she'd intended to invade and conquer the shifter lands, thinking the packs volatile and unable to work together as a unit. With a foothold in the northern part of the realm and the packs decimated, she would have headed south and taken over the rest of Walvashorr."

"But Lorelei and Seth worked together to change that."

Jude scowled now, his arms tight to his chest. "Yes, that's exactly what they did." Lorelei had become Seth's blood rose during the time Jude had helped out. Stunned at how the packs had worked together to destroy so many wraith-pairs, he'd fought in the battle against Margetta until she'd called a retreat.

Hannah reached over and touched his arm. "Hey, if you frown any harder, you'll break your face in half."

He laughed and his arms eased apart.

Suddenly, a soft alarm sounded within the room.

Hannah slid her chair close to the central computer once more and started moving her mouse, then tapping on the keyboard. Her eyes went wide. "Jude, it's from Longeness. He's been trying to reach you."

He'd already removed his coat, which had both the com attached at the shoulder that connected him to the Kellcasse center and his phone. "Shit. Even my phone's in my coat."

"It's okay. I've got your center online. You can video-chat now." She rose from her chair and gestured for him to sit down.

Jude was grateful that when Hannah originally ordered office furniture, she'd planned on accommodating the Vampire

Guardsmen. The three chairs in the room were each built on big lines and could handle his two-eighty and then some.

He sat down and saw his center's com specialist. Longeness rubbed the tip of his right fae ear, pulling all the way to the elongated point, a sure sign of his distress.

Jude knew better than to react. Remaining calm for his people was a constant part of his strategy. "Apologies, Longeness. My phone was elsewhere. What's cookin'?"

"Mastyr, we've had word that another wraith-pair attacked the access checkpoint. The guards survived but only because the pair was intent on getting to the Sound before dawn."

For a long moment, Jude could hardly think. Another wraith-pair was headed toward Port Townsend? They rarely, if ever, crossed the earth access-point lines.

"But that's the second wraith-pair tonight. They never leave Kellcasse." He felt uneasy. He didn't say as much to Longeness, but his first thought went to the ancient fae. Something was on the wind. "Was there anything unusual about this pair? Was a vampire part of the bond and if so, was he a mastyr?"

"Vampire, yes. But to my knowledge, he wasn't a mastyr."

Jude scrubbed a hand through his thick hair, dislodging the clasp. "Well, thank the Goddess for that." Wraith-pairs with mastyr vampires as a mate were nearly impossible to defeat alone. "I'll head out into the Sound and meet these bastards."

"Do you want me to send Guardsmen to back you up?"

"No. I'm good." He'd like to see a regular wraith-pair move against him. "And Longeness, how's the wife?"

"Complaining all the time now." His woman was expecting twins and only had a month to go.

"Completely understandable. Take her some flowers when your shift ends."

"Plan to. I'm not a complete gremlin's ass."

"No, that you're not."

He signed off and grabbed the clasp that now hung at the back of his head, tugging it out in stages. He had an impossible mane of hair, kept long as was the Guardsman's tradition. Thank the elf lords for the invention of crème rinse.

He rose from the chair, lifting his arms to re-clasp his hair, then turned toward Hannah.

She looked odd, though, pressing a hand to her throat. Her gaze tracked the lines of his raised arms and his chest, gradually moving over his hips and down his heavily muscled thighs.

This was one of those moments when he was glad he worked out as much as he did. He knew what he looked like, the raw physical power he exuded because of his size.

And the room suddenly smelled of roses and seashells.

His body heated up something fierce in response because of her perfume. In another minute, if things went on this way, the snug fit of his battle leathers wouldn't be hiding his desire for her.

Securing the woven clasp at the back of his head, he moved toward her. She leaned against the doorjamb, her hands at her sides. "What's going on, Hannah? Why the sudden interest in me?"

"It's not sudden," she whispered, meeting his gaze in that steady way of hers.

"You know this would never work." He drifted his fingers through her hair, still not understanding what had changed that he now wanted Hannah as much as he did.

"I know. You don't do long-term."

"I don't. And your bar is everything to you."

She smiled faintly. "I don't date vampires anyway, you know that. Just humans."

Jude sighed. "Gotta go. I've got a wraith-pair to take down and dawn's about fifteen minutes away."

~ ~ ~

Hannah didn't want to be so completely hooked into Jude right now, but the way he'd talked to Longeness had done something to her. Jude wasn't a simple man by any stretch. She might have been able to shove her interest in him aside if he showed indifference to those around him. Instead, he'd asked about Longeness's very pregnant wife.

She also knew that a long time ago, over a hundred years now, Jude had been married. He'd even had a daughter, but both had died in an Invictus attack. Her email loop had given her a lot of information she wouldn't have had otherwise. She knew they'd perished in his peach orchard on Castle Island, next to the house the couple had built together. Her throat grew tight every time she thought about his loss.

But Jude had never remarried and from that time, he'd kept his relationships on a love-em-and-leave-em basis, yet one more reason she needed to keep her distance and ignore what had become a fairly relentless drive toward him.

Jude made a move to slip past her into the hall, but she caught his arm. "Jude?"

"Yeah?"

"Be careful."

He smiled. "I always am."

Was she imagining things, or had he leaned toward her as if to kiss her.

And she would have let him.

Yep, she had it bad.

But he huffed a quick sigh, and turned up the hall, heading toward the bar. The daytime communication staff would arrive in about three hours, and her staff had already cleaned up and gone home for the night.

She signed off on the loop and added an auto-responder to her email that any emergency communication could be routed through her cell phone. Usually, Sandy came in at this hour to take over, but she had a dentist's appointment so Hannah would be on call until about ten. But like hell she wasn't going to walk down to the nearby dock and watch Jude launch into the air. She was worried now because something didn't feel right.

Moving up the hall toward the bar, she pressed a hand to her chest. She was more anxious about things than she realized because right now her heart felt squeezed tight. She hurried past the horse-shoe shaped bar and a couple dozen tables and chairs toward the entrance. Once there, she stared through the large, stained glass, front door but couldn't believe what she was seeing.

Jude hadn't reached the Sound at all, but fought a wraith-pair not fifty feet from the Gold Rush near the dock.

And the strangest thing of all was that she suddenly felt an overwhelming need to help him. Yet, Jude was one of the most powerful men in all of the Nine Realms, so in what possible situation would he ever need *her* help?

Chapter Two

Flashes of blue battle energy left Jude's palms in steady pulses as the Invictus pair answered with their red strikes.

Hannah had never seen a wraith before or a full-on battle. She'd visited Kellcasse a number of times, but the Invictus, thank God, hadn't shown up.

Her body felt oddly flushed as she watched. Her skin was warm and her hands tingled, as though she was getting ready for something, but for what she had no idea. And strangely, she felt an inexplicable connection to Jude because of these sensations.

Slowly, she opened the door. Jude fought both the wraith and the vampire at the same time – a bonded wraith-pair – levitating, then flying back and forth in quick slashes to avoid being struck. He had some kind of blue shield in front of him as well. It moved with him as he whipped through the air.

The vampire wore battle leathers like Jude's but short boots. His black hair jerked around in lank, beaded strands, and he had a heavy scruff on his face. He held a dagger in his left hand, as if hoping for an opening.

The wraith was a wispy-looking creature, a woman, who wore what looked like a gown of floating red strips of gauze-like fabric. Her limbs appeared elongated, her lips dark, the whites of her eyes yellow.

But it was the shrieking that distressed Hannah the most, a piercing cry that made her cover her ears. The wraith's mate was Guard-sized but still not as big as Jude, but then few Guardsmen she'd met could compete with his mass.

The wraith suddenly flew straight up, then met Hannah's gaze. In a swift streak of movement, she headed straight for Hannah with an intense expression that made Hannah think the wraith had come for her. Why would that ever be true?

Dread assaulted her.

She didn't have time to think or to do anything.

And in that horrible moment, Hannah knew that death had found her.

But just as the wraith would have reached her, a streak of blue struck the wraith's back. She arched in the air, shrieked, then fell hard not five feet from Hannah. She was dead, her back obliterated.

Hannah put her hand to her mouth. The smell of burned flesh nauseated her.

Hannah's gaze moved past the wraith and back to Jude. And as if time had slowed, she watched in horror as Jude fell to the earth as well, the front of his shirt smoking. The mated-vampire, thank God, faltered as well, then hit the pavement with a thud, rolled once and fell unconscious.

She ran to Jude, not caring what happened to either the wraith or her bonded vampire-mate

Jude lay ten feet from the dock, breathing hard, his stomach sliced open, blood pouring from the wound. The same rancid smell of burned flesh caused her to weave on her feet.

His eyes were closed, and he breathed in small pants.

"Jude." She knelt beside him, wanting to touch and comfort him but afraid anything she did right now would cause him pain. She rubbed his arm. "You're hurt."

"I'm fine. I'm healing as we speak, but thank the Goddess you're okay. The wraith?" He tried to look around but she could tell each movement hurt.

Hannah twisted to look behind her. "She's dead."

"Good. If her mate isn't gone as well, he will be soon."

Hannah glanced at the prone vampire who had one leg bent at a strange angle. "He's still breathing, but not moving." She knew that once either part of a wraith-pair died, the remaining mate often followed, especially if wounded in battle as the vampire had been.

Jude winced. "Hannah, listen, I'm in trouble here. I need you to call Longeness. I won't be able to move by myself and the sun's coming up."

To her eye, it was pitch black out, but she'd been around both the light sensitive fae and vampires from the time she could remember and knew that they had internal clocks that counted down the rising sun to the split-second. A vampire caught in the light, even a faint and very distant dawn, would end up burned and blistered. She'd seen the results more than once and it wasn't pretty.

She pulled her phone from her pocket and glanced toward the street. Familiar lights flashed from a Port Townsend police car. The wraith's shrieking had probably prompted some of her neighbors to make a complaint and she couldn't blame them.

Hannah made her call and when Longeness answered, she spoke quietly. "Jude's been hurt and there's a dead wraith nearby and a vampire on his way out as well. The police have shown up, which is never good, and I'll deal with them, but I need to get Jude inside before the sun comes up and I don't know what to do. His Guardsmen have long since returned to Kellcasse."

"Hannah, don't worry. I called for Fleet support as soon as I heard that a wraith-pair had breached the access point. You should be seeing them any second." Kellcasse had a large boat-based policing fleet that patrolled the hundreds of waterways in the realm but which also worked the access point and often entered Sound waters when needed.

"Oh, thank God, and yes, I see the ship now. They're moving at a fast clip."

Jude gripped her hand. "How we doin'? What did Longeness say?"

Hannah had never seen him look so pale. She could feel by the way he held her hand just how much pain he endured. "The Kellcasse Coast Guard is here."

"Thank the Goddess."

The sound of boots on the pavement, coming from the direction of the street, forced Hannah to lift her gaze. A light shined in her face and a scowling policeman stared down at her. "Well, this is a fine mess, Hannah. We've got plenty of people who don't like *their kind* in our town. And now this, a bloody air battle. You're not helping your reputation by sheltering these assholes."

Hannah had gone to school with this idiot who now shined his light at Jude's head. She let go of Jude's hand and rose to her feet. "You know what, Brett," she said, keeping her voice low. "If you don't cut the attitude, I'll tell everyone what you did in your patrol car. Remember?"

His forehead pulled back and his lips formed a thin, tight line, but he didn't say anything else. He shifted his gaze out into the Sound. "Well I can see that Mastyr Jude has a crew coming in. Just make sure they get rid of the bodies. I don't want to have to take any of this slime to my morgue."

He didn't wait for her to respond but turned on his heel and started barking orders at his partner and rounding up the civilians, sending them on their way.

She dropped down beside Jude again. He wore a half-smile and said, "Blackmail. I like it."

"That's all *his kind* deserves."

"What is it you hold over him?" He hissed after getting this sentence out.

"He has a thing for the pros. I was headed home one night, and he'd parked on my street, getting it on in the back seat with a working girl. I may not know all the city rules but I'm pretty sure that was against the law on more than one level."

Jude started to laugh, then groaned.

She shifted her gaze to the dock. The boat was still a ways off, but coming in fast. "Your crew is about half-a-minute away."

"Good."

She glanced at the dying vampire and realized that he'd moved. She lifted up, and saw that his hand, with a red glow in the center of his palm, was aimed in her direction. Oh, God, no!

Without thinking, she threw herself on top of Jude. At the same time, she felt a wave of heat flowing through her that seemed to come from deep within her own body, but had to have come from Jude. She tingled all over as the wave left her. She heard the vampire shout, but she didn't feel any pain. Had his hand-blast struck her in a way that she couldn't feel the damage?

She sat up, aware that she'd just caused Jude a mountain of pain by landing on him. He couldn't seem to catch his breath, and he'd arched his neck. Maybe the vampire had hit his lower extremities with his blast.

She checked Jude, but his legs and boots were fine. So that was good. Glancing back at the vampire, she saw that he looked really strange now and writhed, flipping back and forth, moaning. She rose to her shaky feet and crossed to him. When she drew near, his eyes rolled in his head and his body fell still. Half his clothes were burned off and anywhere his skin showed, she saw ugly blisters. He wouldn't be hurting anyone ever again, but what had caused the burns?

When she returned to Jude, his eyes were closed and his lips compressed.

She heard orders shouted from a small launch that had tied up at the pier. Four trolls leaped onto the dock and started running in her direction.

Trolls had no problem with sunlight and were perfect for rescue missions at dawn or at any time during the day. From the patrol craft, a second boat hit the water shortly after, then a third.

She leaned close to Jude. "Your troops have arrived."

He nodded, just enough, but his eyes were still closed.

"I'm sorry I hurt you."

At that, he turned toward her and squinted up at her. She could tell he wanted to ask her something, but suddenly, the trolls were there. They moved fast on their feet.

"Mastyr, we're here to help."

Jude grunted and tried to move, but she pressed on his shoulder with her hand. She knew he wouldn't like showing weakness of any kind.

"Patience, Hercules," she said, as the trolls got busy with a stretcher. "Even half-gods like you need time to heal when they've gotten a blast wound stretching all the way across the abdomen. And yes, I know how much you hate being laid out like this."

"You got that right." The words were followed with another pained hiss, but she kept her hand on his shoulder, offering resistance the second he tried to move.

"Just concentrate on healing and let these men do their work."

When the lead officer drew close, Jude issued his orders through clenched teeth. He made it clear he was staying at the Gold Rush through the day and that he wanted the coast guard to remain on patrol near the access point until further notice. "Keep Longeness and his crew informed of your movements." He winced as he spoke.

The commander, wearing a stern expression, responded tersely, "Yes, Mastyr." He then turned on a sharp heel and issued orders about the disposal of the wraith-pair, afterward directing eight strong trolls to move Jude carefully onto the stretcher.

And it would take all eight. Trolls were shorter in stature than either the vampire or fae species and then, of course, Jude was … Jude.

He didn't make a sound as they moved him, but blood oozed from his wound, and he'd closed his eyes again, his lips turning white from the pressure once more.

Finally situated on the stretcher, the trolls started moving him swiftly toward the bar. Hannah hurried to the front door and propped it open.

Jude had his arm over his eyes as the trolls carried him inside the building. She was shocked to see that the skin on his cheeks and arms had already started to blister.

So dawn was right on his heels.

As they set him on the floor, she hurried to lower the external steel shutters on the outside of the building. Once down, no light would reach the interior of the space, so that as soon as they were in place, Jude finally relaxed.

He'd started telling the trolls to just leave him there, but Hannah stepped in. "He'll be better off in the bunkroom."

The trolls waited for Jude to nod his acquiescence, then picked up the stretcher once more, moving swiftly toward the rooms at the alley end of the building. Seconds later, Jude lay prone on a broad lower bunk. All the bunks were reinforced with steel to bear the usual Guardsman weight and because the ceiling was open to the duct-work, she'd had the bunks built with a five foot head clearance on the lower bunk.

The commander squatted next to him and Jude spoke in a low tone, thanking him for his crew's quick response and for taking care of the wraith-pair.

Within the next few minutes, the troll unit left by way of the front door. Hannah followed after them, asking the lead troll what precautions would be taken to protect Port Townsend from another attack. The commander assured her that he would have his ship patrolling the stretch of water that linked Port Townsend with the Kellcasse access point throughout the day.

"We'll keep in contact with the Kellcasse Communication Center at all times, but you're not to worry about any of this. We'll keep tabs on the realm-folk who travel today to Port Townsend."

She thanked him for everything. And after taking one last look at the stretchers now hauling away the dead Invictus pair, she locked the front door and returned back to the bunkroom.

Pulling up a low stool, she joined Jude at his bedside. He lay very still, eyes closed.

She remained quiet, waiting. Every once in a while, she'd glance at his abdomen, fascinated to watch the skin knitting together so swiftly. He radiated heat from the energy he spent healing himself, but despite his efforts it seemed to her that he grew paler by the second.

Eventually, his abdomen filled in completely without even a scar remaining to show that he'd been wounded in battle.

He breathed a deep sigh of relief, then sat up, his head easily clearing the bottom of the upper bunk. When Hannah had decided on bunks to save space, she'd had them specially made to accommodate the average size of the Vampire Guard.

He shifted his legs over the side of the bed. Breathing heavily, he leaned forward, his hands clasped loosely between his knees. She could see he was still suffering.

"Do you want me to help you get this shirt off?"

He glanced at her, but his eyes were pinched and bloodshot. "Yes, I'd really like that. The smell—"

"I know."

She moved close, bending over him and lifting his arms carefully to remove the tattered, woven shirt. She threw it in the dust bin.

She'd finally gotten her wish and was now looking at Jude without a shirt on, but she was too troubled to really enjoy the view. She didn't understand why he wasn't doing better.

Healing had definitely used up his resources, but he shouldn't be so pale.

Then she remembered that even if his wounds had disappeared, he still suffered from the chronic pain and cramping from the blood-starvation that all mastyrs endured. From what she understood from the women on the loop, if the mastyrs went too long between feedings they could die.

She swallowed hard. She'd never fed a vampire and it was one of her rules that she never would.

She tried a different tack. "What can I do, Jude? Would you like a sandwich or something? I'm sure I can dig around in the kitchen. Would that help?"

He opened his eyes and met her gaze, his nostrils flaring. He squeezed his eyes shut. "Maybe a beer."

She frowned. Was she really going to have to donate? "I could use one myself. I'll be right back." Could beer hold him off? Of course, she could always call one of her friends who frequently donated to Guardsmen, but again, her fingers started curling up into ugly little balls.

The bar had a number of brews on tap, but she thought a couple of chilled bottles from the fridge would answer better. She went into the storeroom where a few cases were kept in a large refrigerated unit. She pulled out two Tamerland Brown Porters, popped the tops, and headed back to Jude.

His eyes were still closed. And as she dropped down beside him and put a beer in his hand, she'd never seen his skin look so white.

"Sorry," he murmured. "Have to keep my eyes closed for a few more minutes."

She swore she could feel his pain, that though his abdomen was perfectly healed, his stomach was cramping hard.

She looked away from him. She knew what needed to be done and she also knew he'd never ask. But she had the worst feeling that if she gave it up for him, she'd be opening a door that she could never close again.

On the other hand, Jude had just saved her life and had taken a painful hit in the process.

Sitting back down on the stool, she took a long swig of the beer. "Jude, I'm so glad you're okay."

A smiled flickered at the side of his mouth. "Me, too." He tipped the bottle and drank several swallows in a row. "Love this porter."

When he gritted his teeth for about the tenth time, clearly struggling through more hard cramping despite the beer, she resigned herself to what needed to be done.

"Jude, can you open your eyes now?"

He blinked several times. "My vision is better." He turned toward her, but the whites of his eyes were still red, and he squinted. "You okay, Hannah? Because I can't imagine what this was like for you. I'm used to wraiths and battling, but I never wanted you to have to see it."

She thought that the fact he asked her how she was, when he was in so much pain, probably defined Jude's finest quality: He was always thinking of others first.

If she hadn't already made the decision, his concern for her would have pushed her over the edge.

She'd seen humans donate before at the Gold Rush, though Jude had prohibited neck-feeding at the bar. But many vampires took what they needed from the wrist, usually from willing, human females. She also knew that there was a sexual component that couldn't be helped.

Taking a deep breath, she held out her arm and said, "I want to donate."

~ ~ ~

Jude stared down at Hannah's very white wrist and shuddered with need. The blue veins beneath a thin layer of skin called to him like nothing he'd experienced in a long time. His mouth filled with saliva, and his stomach cramped all over again.

Still, he hesitated.

This was Hannah, essentially one of his employees as well as a friend, and he didn't want his relationship disrupted by a blood-feeding. But he hadn't been hurt this bad in a long time.

He'd almost bought it when he turned his battle energy toward the wraith going after Hannah. And when his attention shifted, in that split-second, the wraith's vampire-mate let loose with a powerful strike that had caught him in the gut and opened him up.

But it was seeing Hannah standing there, fully aware she was about to die, that was the real horror. Jude was pretty sure he'd live with that terrifying image in his head for a long time.

And right now, he really didn't like that she was seeing him in a weakened, hungry state. He had a stable of *doneuses* who offered up their blood on a daily basis. He'd chosen these women with great care to make certain that he never developed an attachment or inadvertently created feelings he couldn't return by tapping into a vein. Most of the women were married with families, so their loyalties lay elsewhere.

Donating always carried a certain level of sexual heat, and for that reason he never drank from the throat, which kept that heat at a low, acceptable level. And he never drank from the women he dated. He held to his commitment to remain unattached until the Invictus no longer plagued the Nine Realms.

The trouble was every molecule in his body craved Hannah, from her blood, to her lips, her breasts, her hips. He wanted to bury his cock deep between her legs, to do what he'd been lusting after for months.

And now she was offering up her life-force for his to take.

A big part of him didn't want to. Hannah had become a vulnerability for him this past year, though he couldn't exactly explain why. The encounter in the closet had cracked the door just a bit, but if he drank from her, he suspected he'd be throwing the door wide.

But he needed blood desperately. He hadn't said anything, but his stomach had been spasming for the last half hour so that he could hardly breathe.

The difficult battle, coming at the tail end of a long night, had used up his reserves, as well as the energy required to heal himself and just stay alive. He was close to a point of no return so he couldn't really turn down her offer even if he wanted to. He carried too much responsibility on his shoulders to risk his life on a point of discretion.

But he knew in his gut he shouldn't be doing this.

He met her gaze. "I'm grateful, Hannah. And I accept your offer. I'll never forget this." He would at least try to restrain himself.

She smiled and nodded, encouraging him. "I can feel that you're reluctant and I know why. I know you don't want to disrupt our working relationship. But this one time will be okay. You'll see."

He didn't say anything, but her statement had the feel of *famous last words.*

Still, he followed suit. "And afterward I'll do everything I can to make sure things stay on an even keel."

She dipped her chin once more, her gaze falling to his lips.

He drew a deep breath, "But you'll need to lie down beside me. I don't have the strength to do this sitting up. Okay?"

She looked a little panic-stricken, but she nodded. "Whatever you need is fine by me." Her cheeks were flushed, and her scent that he loved floated in the air now, roses and the seashore.

He lay back down on the bed and scooted toward the wall as she stretched out beside him.

He took her left wrist gently in his right hand, which pulled her body closer to him so that she snuggled in tight. And damn him for loving it.

His chin trembled now. Having made the decision, the scent of her blood reached him, and because he'd been lusting after her, his groin heated up, a reaction he wasn't able to help. He'd been longing for her anyway, but taking her blood sent him into overdrive. He just hoped she understood, because he couldn't exactly hide his arousal.

He hadn't even bitten her arm and he was already hard.

Hannah, he pathed, reaching for her telepathically. He'd communicated this way with her before, many times, usually when he wanted to tease her about something. But this time, he needed to be able to talk to her while he drank.

I hear you, Jude. Her lips were parted and her eyes dilated. Her scent had thickened in the air. The desire was mutual.

You've never been tapped before, right?

She shook her head. *Never.*

So this is a first time.

She nodded, her eyes widening as her gaze settled on her wrist.

Look at my mouth, Hannah. I don't want you to be afraid. I want you to see the whole thing.

She blinked several times, her gaze shifting to his lips.

You might want to adjust your position just a little. He pulled her wrist up to his mouth, helping her to feel how the angle could become uncomfortable for her. She shifted upwards so that he could feel her breasts against his ribs, which did not help at all. She had beautiful, full breasts and she'd caught him having a good long look more than once. But feeling them in such an intimate situation supported the already solid bulge in his leathers.

Feeding will take a few minutes. If you want to lean into me, feel free. My wounds are healed. You won't hurt me.

Okay.

He wrapped his arm around her waist to support her. *You ready?*

Yes.

He lowered his fangs, and a soft groan left her throat. Oh, sweet Goddess, she was into this as much as he was. He understood then that he was in a mountain of trouble.

He'd desired Hannah for months, now here she was, pressed up against his side, her scent wafting through his brain, teasing him, working him up.

And he'd be feeding from her.

~ ~ ~

Hannah saw Jude's fangs emerge and the sight of them had the strangest effect as desire streaked through her abdomen and grabbed her deep between her legs. She didn't understand why, but it didn't matter. All these months of hungering for Jude seemed to coalesce as he arched his neck slightly. Then his fangs sank in a quick strike that she barely felt. Just as blood pooled, his lips formed a seal and he began to suck.

As her blood left her body, the fullness in her chest began to ease. Although, hearing Jude suckle her wrist and watching his lips move in a steady rhythm started making her feel things she'd been repressing for months. She wanted his lips on her breasts doing the same thing, then down low working her with the same tugging motion.

Hannah, he pathed, dragging her gaze from his lips to his beautiful smoky gray eyes. They were dark with need. *What are you thinking about?*

I'm just feeling so much.

I can tell. Your perfume is getting to me, like roses and the seashore.

She smiled. *Is that what I smell like to you?*

Much more than that. I can smell your desire.

She nodded. *Can't help myself.*

I'm feeling it as well. There's always a sexual component to feeding like this. But with you, sweet Goddess—!

Movement by her hips drew her gaze to his well-defined arousal pushing against his pants. The snug battle leathers he wore left nothing to the imagination, and right now she wanted what he had to give. And he was a big man, in every way.

Her mind moved swiftly to what it would be like to unzip his leathers and have a look, a feel, a taste.

Deep within her body, sexual need began to pulse like nothing she'd experienced in her entire life, an intense desire that demanded release.

Do you like what you see? His deep resonant voice, even within her mind, sent new waves pulsing within her abdomen. She slid her gaze back to his eyes. He had a desperate look now, and she felt the same way.

This isn't easy, she pathed. *I've wanted you for months. I've tried not to show it.* Dangerous words. She should pull it back, stop feeding this fire.

I've wanted you as well. I've craved you, Hannah.

She was losing control as she nodded. *It felt very mutual, both of us pretending.*

He sucked harder now, and his breathing had grown rough. *Hannah, I know this isn't right, but I'd give anything if you would touch me. Do you think you could do that?*

Yes, I can. I want to so bad.

Even within her mind, he sounded as desperate as she felt, but the position was awkward. Her other hand was caught between her body and his, so she began to maneuver, freeing her arm. When she had her shoulder planted against his side, she was at a good angle. He helped by holding her wrist higher.

She slid her hand downward and the next thing she knew, she connected through the leather with what was hard.

The groan that came out of Jude was heavy and prolonged. Her own desire rose like a heavy, ocean wave, lifting her up, then casting her onto the shore. She wanted this, she wanted him, and she wanted it now.

She began massaging him, while at the same time arching her hips against his thigh. God, she needed some friction.

I'm in agony. Jude, I've wanted you so badly. My body is on fire. And your beautiful chest, your pecs, your abs –

Hannah, look at me.

Feverish now as he sucked on her wrist, as he drank her blood, she shifted her gaze back to his eyes.

His voice penetrated her mind once more. *Hannah.*

She heard the pleading tone in his voice, and she knew she shouldn't, but she'd been holding back for months. They were alone; all the doors locked up tight.

Hannah, I want to make love to you.

Her rational, sensible reasons for keeping her distance somehow vanished. Then she nodded, her voice betraying her. "Yes."

He released her wrist, swiping the wounds to heal them. He was still breathing hard as he leaned up on his elbows. She moved onto her knees positioning herself at his waist, then worked at his leathers.

When she started to unzip he said, "Careful. I go commando."

Hannah's fingers trembled, but not from fear. She'd never been so overcome in her life, her whole body aching to do this with Jude. She slid her fingers beneath the zipper so that as she pulled the tab down, she protected his cock.

It felt so strange to feel his hardness beneath her fingers while she unzipped.

This was Jude.

She looked back at his face, at his swollen lips and glazed eyes. His nostrils flared. His clasp had come undone and with his massive hair hanging around his shoulders and down to his waist, he looked wild and ferocious.

She felt dizzy and aroused beyond anything she'd ever imagined. Reverting her attention to his zipper, she carefully peeled back his pants and freed his arousal.

She took a moment to just look at him, then glided her thumb and forefinger from the top of his crown over his ridge, and all the way to the base of his stalk. He groaned.

She leaned down and took the head in her mouth, loving the velvety feel against her tongue.

Jude's hips moved in a slow familiar rhythm. His breathing had grown even more ragged. "Hannah, wait."

She understood and released him. Getting back to the task at hand, she moved to his thigh boots, the ones she'd been wanting to touch for months now.

She slid her fingers down both sides, touching each of the silver medallions. They bore the stamped image of the eagle, a prominent predator in the Pacific Northwest. She found the zipper on the inside and peeled the boot off his right leg then the other.

Her heart pounded now as she slowly worked his leathers off. He reached for her often, grazing her shoulder, her cheek, her hair with his fingers. The whole time he remained aroused, calling to her. She ached with need. But she didn't go fast, knowing she would probably never do this again with Jude.

It was a one-time-only deal.

His beautiful scent filled her nostrils as she stared down at his warrior's body. She drew close and with her hand took a journey up his left leg, his thigh, his groin, his abdomen, his pecs. Then she leaned close and caught his chin in hand. "Jude, will you let me do something for you?"

His brows rose, questioning, but he nodded.

She smiled. "I'll be right back." She wasn't sure what had prompted her to do this, but she moved into the bathroom, ran the faucet over several washcloths, wrapped them up in a towel, then returned to his bunk.

Setting the towel next to him, she began bathing him and his whole body relaxed. "Damn, that feels good and I'm not even sure why. What made you think of it?"

"I don't know." She made a pass over his muscular chest, savoring not just his physical body but all that he was. "I just had a feeling this would be the right thing to do. And … well, it's my way of thanking you for saving my life and for sacrificing for your people every night of your life."

Chapter Three

Jude watched Hannah work her way down his legs with the damp terry-cloth. Even though he wanted her beneath him, her body writhing with each thrust of his cock, he wouldn't have missed this for the world. It felt sacred and beautiful, more Hannah than she knew.

Watching her bathe even his feet, eased something deep inside him. He'd been making war for so long without a woman at his side that he'd forgotten what it could be like.

When she was done, she took the towel into the bathroom and busied herself for a moment, probably hanging out each of the cloths to dry separately. She'd get after the men for not keeping the bathroom in order.

But when she returned, his heart almost stopped.

She had nothing on.

He rose up on his elbows as she approached the bed slowly, her nipples peaked, the way they'd been in the stockroom that day. He wanted to be suckling her.

He could feel that bathing him had aroused her, which kept him hard as hell knowing that she enjoyed touching him. Maybe this had been a fantasy of hers. He'd had plenty of fantasies himself since that supply-room day, and she'd just fulfilled one of them.

She stopped at the foot of the bunk. He looked her up and down slowly and she let him look. "When you finally fall into bed after a night's work, do you think of me, Hannah? Did you once imagine doing this with me in the bunkroom?"

She met his gaze, her lips parted and swollen. "Not the bathing part, but groping you, yes. Does that shock you?"

He smiled, and his hips arched. "I've imagined doing the same thing to you, usually when I first wake up."

A soft moan left her throat, and for a moment she closed her eyes as though seeing new images she'd want to remember later.

"Oh, Jude," she murmured, as she opened her eyes. Her gaze fell to his cock once more. "And would you be touching yourself when you thought of me?"

"Uh-huh."

She moved to stand next to the bunk. "Show me. I want to watch."

He settled his left hand on her waist and with his right took hold of his cock. He stroked slowly, his hips undulating, but his gaze was fixed on her.

Her eyes fell to half-mast as she leaned down and took him in her mouth again.

"Oh, Hannah. Sweet Goddess." He could come like this, one hand on his cock, her lips on his head, and his hand now drifting to fondle her ass.

"Spread your legs. Let me feel you."

The moment she responded, he slid his hand even lower and gently began touching what was wet and smelled of roses and the ocean. He wanted his mouth there.

"I want to taste you while you're sucking me. Straddle me, Hannah."

Jude, slid through his mind. But she didn't hesitate.

She climbed up on the bed, facing away from him. And right then, he was glad she'd had the bunks built with a lot of clearance.

He caught her right leg, easing it to the far side, so that she faced away from him. With her legs spread, her beautiful scent hit him full force and he grunted, anxious to taste her. He caught her hips, bringing her down to him.

At the same time that he laid his tongue over her clitoris, she took his cock in her mouth once more.

He arched. The dual sensation of his tongue licking what was wet and swollen and her mouth suckling him, brought his balls up tight. He could come so easily, but he controlled himself, forcing his body to settle down. He'd imagined doing this to Hannah, just as he'd said, but he'd never dreamed that he'd actually get the chance.

When he drove his tongue deep inside her well, she lifted up, crying out, "Jude, oh God!"

He realized she was close and he wanted her to come. He added a soft realm vibration through his tongue, which set her to writhing. Using his hands to hold her hips in place, he plunged in and out vampire fast. She shuddered then cried out repeatedly as she released.

He kept working her, savoring the pulses deep within, and that she panted, her hips rocking in swift jerks until the last of her ecstasy faded.

After a minute, she finally eased down. "Jude, that was amazing. But did I actually feel a vibration? I mean I've heard the gossip."

"Yes, you did."

He smiled as he caressed her bottom, kissing her all over. The thought went through his head that he could stay in this position, loving on her, for a long time.

She spoke quietly. "So, how do you want me?"

Here, for the next twelve months.

"Oh…" The word came out breathless. "Sounds like a plan. But you know what I really want right now?"

"Anything. I'll do anything." And he meant it.

"Your cock, buried deep."

Her words launched him.

With a generous distance to the upper bunk, he was able to rise up, half-levitating to make the move. He held her in the same position, coming up behind her so that she landed on her hands and knees. He pushed her hair away from her neck. "I want to feed from you here, Hannah, from this vein." He stroked her neck. "And I want to do it while I make you come."

"Jude, I would love that." Her body writhed against him. "I didn't know donating would feel as good as it does, as sexual, but it's amazing."

He took his cock in hand, positioning himself at her entrance. "Do you like how this feels? My cock right here, ready to penetrate?"

"Yes. Oh, God, yes."

He smiled as he took her hips in his hands and began to push. He'd imagined this as well, but the reality was a thousand times better than the fantasy, and the fantasy had rocked.

He drove into her, then pulled back. She moaned and made soft shuddering sounds. "You're so big. You fill me."

He loved that he could please her like this.

Once he was fully seated and had established a steady rhythm, he leaned over her and murmured against her cheek, "I'm going to bite you again, Hannah. Would you like that? Then I'm going to add some vibration right here." He gave her a solid thrust.

"You can do that?"

"Yes. I can."

~ ~ ~

"Oh, Jude." Shivers traveled up and down her body. She'd been aching for this kind of contact for months. Now here Jude was and then some.

She might have imagined his size before in her frequent fantasies, but he'd not only exceeded expectation, he just told her he could add vibration deep inside her.

She clenched hard at the thought.

She was on her hands and knees and Jude was thrusting, continuously hitting her just right. Her lips were parted as she dragged in air between pants. With one hand, he smoothed away her hair to expose her throat.

She felt his body angle over her back and with one arm pressed against her breasts, he supported her. His tongue swept over her neck repeatedly. He made a hungry sound with his mouth, guttural and coarse, more animal-like than man, and she loved it.

When he caused her vein to rise, only something a vampire could do, she pushed back with her hips.

I'm going to bite you now.

Yes. Please, yes.

The sting was brief and the moment he began to suck her blood once more, a wave of pleasure hit her like nothing she'd known. The passion came from the depths of her being and flowed into her mind. She soon felt drugged and euphoric at the same time.

And still he thrust, a steady powerful drive, full of mastery. Was this really happening?

His sucking became agitated.

What is it?

I'm so damn close, Hannah, but I want you to come again.

Just slow things down a bit, okay?

She felt him take a deep breath, and move into her with gentler thrusts. *Yes, that's better. And when you can, how about that vibration?*

Absolutely.

But he surprised her when suddenly she felt a vibration not between her legs, but at her neck where he fed from her.

Shivers once more chased each other down her neck, ramping up her need and intensifying the feel-good between her legs. *I love that your world is full of vibrations. I just never thought … this would happen … to me … oh, you're doing it now. My God.* She'd barely been able to get the words out, because he'd just added an intoxicating vibration through his cock. At the same time, she felt a wonderful warmth that added yet another layer of sensation.

She moaned heavily. "Jude, the heat and vibration together. I won't last long."

Good, because I'm ready. I want to fill you up, Hannah.

I want to be filled.

While still suckling at her vein, he drove with purposeful, deep thrusts and the vibration kept getting stronger. She gulped in air, panting hard. She felt her orgasm hovering, but she wanted to hold back, and was unwilling to let go just yet because of all the exquisite sensations.

But when he began to move his hips fast, curling them in quick thrusts, her body took over. A great swell began inside her, taking her breath away. Pleasure unfurled as she pulled hard on Jude's cock, intensifying her desire. The heat and the vibration grew stronger, amplifying what she felt, building to a pinnacle.

Suddenly, the release flew from her, and she cried out as a warm, heady flush engulfed her body, forcing her to writhe heavily against Jude. Her heart felt lit on fire. She moaned, then once again cried out over and over at the intensity of the orgasm.

Hannah, what you're doing to me!

It's unbelievable. The sweet, gripping sensation kept rolling, and just when it peaked and she thought she was through, Jude began to release, igniting pleasure all over again.

His cock, still vibrating, pistoned within her, and another orgasm swelled, streaking through her, gaining in size and heat, then once more flooding her body with so much pure ecstasy and so many sensations that this time she screamed. She could hardly catch her breath as he continued to drive into her, as he shouted into the air, as his cock released his seed in pulses.

The orgasm swirled through her, forcing small cries from her mouth again and again, until at last she began to ease back from the pinnacle.

It was some time before she came to an awareness that Jude was no longer moving and that he'd released her neck and was now kissing her over and over above her vein. *Thank you, Hannah. This was an amazing experience. I swear, I've never had a release like that before.*

Her mind felt muddled. She wanted to tell him she hadn't either, but this made her laugh softly because nothing about making love with him was exactly in her catalog of prior experiences. Nothing could compare.

Of course, now her arms shook from staying in one position so long. She chuckled again. "I need to lie down."

He lowered her slowly and because he was big, he remained connected to her which she thought absolute genius.

"Let me know if I get too heavy."

"K." She drew in a deep breath. She still felt drugged out and sleepy at the same time. She really needed to head to bed for the day.

She closed her eyes, reaching for Jude's hand. When she found it, she clasped his fingers tight. "Thank you."

She felt him sigh. He was a solid weight on top of her, even though he held himself up on his forearms. He felt so good. He'd remained half-aroused, which made her wiggle a couple of times just to feel him.

But as she lay there, sweat began to trickle down her forehead. She was really perspiring, something that made sense given what she'd just been through and yet didn't. In fact, she felt warm all over, and she could tell her temperature was climbing in a very bizarre way.

"Jude, something's wrong. Get off. Please. I'm sorry, but I think I'm in trouble."

Jude pulled out of her then moved backwards. She slid sideways from the bunk then headed straight to the bathroom where she quickly started up the shower, though leaving the temp on cold.

She heard him follow after her, his bare feet padding on the tile floor.

"Hannah, did I hurt you?"

"No, of course not. This is … I don't what this is. I'm just over-heated in a way that is really off."

She stepped into the cool spray, and groaned because it felt so good. She dipped her head under the water, savoring the icy feel. But how strange that she actually liked the temperature. She should have been jumping and shouting because it was so cold.

Instead, heaven.

Yet her whole body seemed to be on fire. Did having sex with a vampire do this to a human? Or feeding a vampire maybe?

She'd had plenty of friends who'd crawled into bed with vampires, even donated from a willing vein. But she'd never had one tell her she felt like her body had become a living inferno.

When she finally felt cool enough, she stepped from the shower and wrapped herself up in a towel.

Jude had remained by the door. And as naked as he was, with just his long mane of black hair surrounding his muscular shoulders and arms, he'd never looked sexier.

She almost suggested a second round, but he stared at her with an odd expression, his gray eyes wide and a frown between his brows. "Hannah, what's going on? You look like you're sunburned, stem to stern."

She turned and looked at herself in the mirror over the sink. He was right. She was very flushed. She glanced down at her legs and toes. Same thing.

Shifting to face Jude once more, she shook her head. "Do you think I might have some kind of allergy to you, because I can't explain this heat at all. Or is it something that occasionally happens to your donors?"

He shook his head, his frown deepening. "Never." After a long moment, she grew uncomfortable with the way he kept staring at her. He looked worried. "Okay, what's going on?"

"I'm not sure. But, I do have a question. Can you tell me how you felt after I fed from your wrist?"

She spread her hands wide. "Good. I mean a lot better, actually. I'd had this kind of weight on my chest." Something about that sounded familiar, but her mind wouldn't bring anything into sharp focus. "Afterward, though, I was just fine."

~ ~ ~

Jude stood rooted to the floor. He'd finally realized that something very realm was going on with Hannah.

He took deep breaths because he was afraid of what was coming next and he didn't want to look at it, not even a little. "I should head back to Kellcasse." A completely irrational statement given that the sun was up. But, yeah, he wanted to run.

She chuckled. "You can't go. You'd be fried to a pile of ashes."

He nodded. She was right, but she was still bright red, beautiful as hell with her violet eyes glittering and her damp hair drawn away from high cheekbones. But still her skin was such an odd shade. "I know."

"Jude, you look distressed."

He closed his eyes. He didn't want to think about this or to acknowledge any of its truth. He knew this particular phenomenon was racing through the Nine Realms, perhaps even in response to Margetta's aggression against their world, but it couldn't happen to him. Not now. Not ever.

He couldn't have a permanent woman in his life. He'd lost his wife and daughter and that had been it for him, his last attempt at normalcy while he was ruler of Kellcasse. He was too much of a target and Naomi's death, as well as Joy's, had been a deliberate attack against him.

Yes, he had a powerful reason for remaining unattached.

Putting his hand to his stomach, he groaned, not because of the usual cramping but because it was gone, completely gone. He was pain-free for the first time since he'd gained mastyr status so long ago.

And to his knowledge, there was only one reason he could ever be free of that kind of pain.

He opened his eyes, meeting Hannah's now-worried gaze. She'd taken a couple of steps closer. "Jude, what's going on?"

"Did you ever wonder why you were suddenly so into me in the same way I'd become obsessed with making more frequent trips to the Gold Rush?"

She shrugged. "I guess I just thought I'd awakened to this." She waved a hand to encompass his entire body. She even smiled.

In any other circumstance, he would have been gratified, his male ego stroked nicely by her words. He would have smiled as well, maybe even laughed, and he definitely would have hauled her back into his arms.

But not this time.

Things had just gotten way too complicated.

"Think, Hannah. You said your heart felt weighty until you fed me. Doesn't that sound familiar to you? I know that you're on the loop with all the other bonded females. Surely they've talked about what it's like for them."

She laughed and used a second towel to pat her hair dry. "But you're talking nonsense now."

"Am I?"

"Of course. Look, I think you're overreacting to what happened between us just now." She waved in the direction of the bunkroom. "You know, in there. And it was amazing."

For a moment, he let himself remember, and his tension eased a little. "It was incredible."

She cocked her head. "Wait a minute. I just supposed it was always like that for you."

He shook his head. "No. This was damn extraordinary."

At that, she frowned. "You mean the sex?"

"Especially the sex. What did you think I meant?"

"The feeding, of course."

"That, too." His gaze fell to her neck and an internal vibration very deep wanted to rise, one that he'd kept suppressed for a hundred years. Shit, this couldn't be happening, but all the signs were there. Yet, Hannah wasn't taking his hints.

"I need to ask you something."

Hannah leaned her hips against the sink, the second towel bunched in her hands. She looked troubled, and her gaze flitted toward him then away. "Sure. Whatever."

"Why did you throw yourself on me like you did, earlier, in the parking lot? At the time, I didn't understand because it hurt like hell. So why did you?"

"You don't know what happened?" She set the towel on the sink, then tightened the one around her body.

"Only that you seemed to be protecting me," Jude said. "But from what I still don't know. I was flat on my back and I couldn't see everything that was going on."

Her eyes widened. "Well, because that vampire was aiming his hand-blast at you. I was looking back at the dock and caught sight of this red glow and it was coming from his palm. He would have killed you so I covered you."

"Shit," he murmured.

She then shook her head. "But Jude, don't you remember what happened next, because you sent this kind of wave of heat passing right through me and it burned him up. He was horribly blistered and died soon after. Don't you remember? Didn't you see what you did to him?"

Jude's spirits sank one more notch. She'd just confirmed everything in those few words. It was also clear she didn't understand what had really happened. "I don't have that kind of power to bring fire out of my body and destroy others, to burn others."

She put both hands on her head. "I'm so confused. I don't get what you're saying. How is that possible? I mean maybe what happened was that your usual blasting power got activated somehow."

"If it had passed through you, you'd be dead. No, Hannah, I had nothing to do with killing that vampire." He could see she was in a state of shock as she slowly lowered her arms to her sides.

"If you're suggesting that *I* had anything to do with it, I think you're crazy. I run a bar, I don't kill vampires."

"But you did and I think it's tied up with the flush that's finally fading from your skin."

She looked away from him, shaking her head. "None of this makes sense."

Jude said nothing more, but waited for her to catch up. His mind rolled inward and switched lanes completely as he recalled being in Walvashorr with Mastyr Seth, and so deeply attracted to Lorelei, Seth's emerging blood rose.

Jude had heard the tales, about the level of possessiveness a mastyr would feel for his woman and the drive he'd have toward her, but he'd dismissed a good portion of this as outright embellishment.

Until … and he cringed at the memory … until he'd found himself alone with Lorelei for the first time. It was as though he'd lost his mind. He went after her and something about her blood-rose state responded to his mastyr status as well. She'd all but opened her arms to him.

The moment had ended with Seth attacking him and he and Seth would have battled to the death if Lorelei hadn't intervened.

As he stared at Hannah, he knew he'd just gotten thrown into the deep end once more. If she was a blood rose, or an emerging one, with unique incredible powers, and she remained unbonded for any length of time, *every mastyr* in the Nine Realms would eventually come hunting her.

He'd take the chronic pain he suffered as a mastyr to be rid of this horrible situation. He didn't want a Goddess be-damned woman in his life, he hadn't asked for a blood rose, and like hell he was going to act on it.

But this was Hannah. And if he wasn't careful, a mastyr vampire of lesser ability and no character at all, could seduce her. Then she'd be locked into a life of pure torture.

What the hell was he supposed to do?

~ ~ ~

Hannah could feel that for whatever reason, Jude's anger had taken over. Though why he was mad, she wasn't sure.

Of course, nothing made sense to her right now. It was almost as though she knew something in the very center of her brain, but she couldn't bring herself to look at it.

She glanced down at her toes once more, now more pink than red, so the flush was fading.

But what had caused all the redness?

Her tingling hands were still really warm and bugging her. She rubbed them together again.

And Jude had no pain.

She mentally danced a little more.

Maybe this was simple. She'd fed him and something about feeding him had been a little different than what he was used to. That had to be it. And as for her killing a vampire, well, he'd lost a whole bag of screws on that one. She was more likely to shut the Gold Rush down forever than to even kill a flea. All spiders walked out of her bar alive.

With her towel still snug, she turned toward the sink and flipped on the cold water. She held her hands beneath the stream and felt some relief from the tingling. Maybe it was time to see a doctor.

Jude drew close and settled a gentle hand on her shoulder. "Hannah."

Why did he sound so resigned? And to what?

She held her hands up for him to see. "My hands won't cool down, even though the water is freezing. I shouldn't have fed you. This is because I fed you. I knew I shouldn't have. I'm human, you're realm and we shouldn't engage like that."

"I know this is hard for you."

She slammed the faucet off, wiping her hands on the towel still wrapped around her, then whirled toward him. "What do you mean, this must be hard?"

But his gray eyes were filled with so much compassion that she took a step back, bumping into the sink. "Stop looking at me like that."

"Hannah."

"And stop speaking my name with such remorse. I donated happily. You're my friend. Why wouldn't I have done so?"

"This isn't about your having fed me. And your body isn't flushed because you opened a vein. Don't you see?"

She stared at him, but kept shaking her head.

"Hannah."

"No." She held up both hands as though to ward him off.

Suddenly, the whirling in her brain stopped so that she finally had to stare at an enormous central monolith that had two words chiseled on it, all in caps: BLOOD ROSE.

"No," she cried out.

She knew what it meant. She'd heard the women talk about how much their lives had changed and that was the last thing she wanted.

Jude caught her in his arms and held her.

"I don't want this, Jude. I'm not that person. I love you as one of my dearest friends, but I'm human. I'm human." She clung to his massive shoulders and started sobbing. It was all too much, her lust and longing for him, her respect for him, the sex that had just rocked her world. "I don't understand how I could be a blood rose."

"Abigail was human."

Hannah drew back and stared up at Jude, though she still held tightly to him like an anchor in heavy seas. "And now she's a vampire. Is that what I'll become?"

"Not necessarily, at least, I don't think so. Sweet Goddess, I don't know. But I do think you're becoming realm."

She held out her hands and glanced from one palm to the other. "What is this, Jude? Why do my hands tingle? Why does my body grow so warm and flushed?" She drew in a long, slow breath.

Then she remembered when Jude had begun his vibration between her legs that she'd felt all this warmth and she now knew that heat had come from her. Oh, God.

But one more horrible thought intruded. "Did I really kill that vampire?"

Jude nodded slowly.

The thought that she had taken a life, even one that needed to be brought down, caused her to tremble.

Jude pulled her close once more. "I'm so sorry, Hannah."

She let him comfort her for a moment, then pulled out of his arms. "You don't understand. This bar is my life. I ended my last long-term relationship because my ex wanted me to give up the Gold Rush, to sell it, just to be with him."

"I know. I remember."

She planted a hand against her chest. "The Gold Rush is who I am."

"I know. By all the elf-lords, I do know who you are. But we're in trouble here, Hannah. Please tell me you understand. I didn't ask for this and I definitely would never have wished this on you in a million years, but we're here and we're in trouble." He then reminded her of what each of the bonded women would have already told her, that she would be pursued heavily by other mastyr vampires.

She put a hand to her forehead. "Oh, God. This can't be happening. And I'm so unfit for anything like that. I thought I was performing a good-enough service here, giving you men a place to chill and even to sleep over, not to mention running the communications center. So why wasn't that enough that somehow the powers of your world have descended on me? I just don't get it."

"I don't know, either, but I do know someone who can help, who can give us some answers."

Hannah began to relax. "Vojalie."

Jude nodded. "Tell you what. Let me contact her and see if we can meet up tonight." He glanced around. "How about at your house at full-dark?"

She couldn't help the tears that rolled down her cheeks. "Sounds like a plan."

She watched Jude move back into the bunkroom, pull out his locker and slip into a pair of boxers. He then sat down on the side of the bed and turned inward, eyes closed. From the energy she felt radiating from him, she knew he'd connected with either Vojalie or her husband, Davido. Most realm-folk didn't have that kind of power to hold a telepathic conversation realm-to-realm. Jude did, as did all the other mastyrs of the Nine Realms, which was one reason power-levels defined the mastyr-status. The most powerful mastyr in each realm ruled. Simple.

When Jude finally relaxed and looked up at her, she knew the call had ended.

"What's the word?" she asked.

"Both Vojalie and Davido will join us at your house at full-dark. Sound good?"

Hannah finally breathed a sigh of relief. "Like the best possible news."

He stood up and took her gently by the shoulders. "Don't worry. We'll figure something out."

Hannah wasn't quite as hopeful as Jude appeared to be, but she nodded. "I really need my bed. How about you?"

"Yep." He kissed her once, a brief warm kiss, after which she put her clothes back on and left the bunkroom. Jude needed his sleep as much as she did.

She returned to the communication center and made arrangements to have one of her workers, Greg, take over until Sandy arrived from her dental appointment.

When Greg had settled in, Hannah walked up the hill to her home, a climb that she usually enjoyed but which felt about a mile long given all that she'd been through.

By the time she fell into bed, sleep roared toward her and she embraced it with open arms.

~ ~ ~

Later that evening, after Hannah had shared wine with her guests, she invited Vojalie to join her on the roof deck that overlooked the Sound. In older days, this would have been called 'the widow's walk'. When the sun shined, Hannah often came here to lay out and try to pink up her very white, Pacific Northwest skin, usually without much success.

Vojalie had already admired the view and thanked her for the lovely Cabernet Sauvignon. She then asked Hannah to give her a brief history of the current situation with Jude and what appeared to be a strange realm gift that had come to her so unexpectedly.

Hannah quietly outlined the details, including how and when her interest in Jude had suddenly exploded. Vojalie even smiled at the supply closet scenario.

She explained as best she could about how she seemed to have some kind of power that had released as a wave of heat and killed a vampire.

Vojalie lifted her brows this time.

After Hannah was done, Vojalie remained looking out to sea for a long time, her forearms on the railing. Peace radiated from the beautiful fae woman who was probably the most powerful of her kind in the Nine Realms.

She wasn't quite as tall as Hannah and had very fae features with a thin nose and a strong pointed chin. She wore a lavender headband holding back her long, dark brown hair. Her equally dark eyes glimmered with a mountain of compassion. Though she'd never seen it before, she knew that Vojalie's eyes would turn silver when she enthralled someone, usually while seeking information.

She was definitely the woman to ask for help and counsel.

After a time, Vojalie turned toward her. "First, you have what is known as a fire-gift and it's extremely rare. I haven't seen it in centuries, in fact, but you have all the hallmarks. I would imagine you find cold water soothing."

"Very. But what does this mean?"

Vojalie shrugged. "It's no doubt connected to your being a blood rose, but I have a feeling its purpose is specific and will be made known to you within the next few days or weeks even. Although the fact that you saved Jude's life is a hint all on its own."

“So I’m a fiery blood rose.”

Vojalie smiled. “You could say that.” But her expression soon became serious as she continued, “All nine of the ruling mastyrs have carried an enormous load for centuries. And I’ve been hoping for a long time that something very realm would one day arrive to relieve their suffering. I just never thought it would be the blood rose phenomenon. It has occurred before in our history, but in such distant times that I actually had to look it up in the ancient documents. But these men … they’re so deserving.”

Hannah sighed. “Jude especially. He’s done so much for his realm, which is one reason I’m as upset as I am. Jude should have a blood rose in his life, just not me. And you know I love realm-folk. I’ve essentially grown up around them, and I’ve known Jude since I was a child.”

Hannah rubbed what she knew to be a frown between her brows. “What I’m trying to say, is that the way I feel has little to do with Jude and more to do with how much I’d be giving up.”

“You feel you’d have to give up the Gold Rush.”

“And my home, my friends, my entire way of life. I’m not ignorant of just how much each of the lives of the current bonded blood roses has changed.”

Vojalie cocked her head, her eyes narrowing slightly. “I’m wondering though, if there isn’t something more going on here. Is it possible your feelings are cloaked with events from the past? Bad experiences?”

Hannah could see that Vojalie’s eyes had turned silver, a sure sign of enthrallment, but it didn’t bother Hannah at all. Instead, she found herself telling Vojalie all about her ex, Mark Jackson, and his control issue. “And I know Jude likes things the way he likes them.”

"Well that he does, as most men do. But it also sounds to me like your ex had a much deeper issue than Jude could possibly have. I believe, and you make take it for what it's worth, that your Mr. Jackson will one day become an abuser, if not physically then emotionally. I imagine while you were together, he helped you to feel very small about the choices you made for your life."

Vojalie had said it exactly right. "As though his were important and mine weren't."

"You were wiser than you knew when you parted company with him."

To a degree, Hannah already knew that Vojalie was right. But hearing her suspicions supported out loud helped a lot.

Vojalie asked, "So, how does Jude feel about what's happened?"

"Actually, I'm not sure which of us is more distressed."

Vojalie frowned slightly. "I believe he must be thinking about his wife and daughter. You know about them, right? The lovely Naomi and their daughter, Joy?"

Hannah nodded.

Vojalie's silver eyes appeared haunted as she looked into the past. "We were all devastated when we heard the news. Did you know they'd been killed in the small, peach orchard on Jude's property? On Castle Island?"

"Yes, but that's all I really know and I never probed for details."

"No, of course not." Vojalie gave herself a shake. "Now, I don't mean to make you uncomfortable, but there are a few things I must know. You've made love with Jude, right?"

Maybe it was the enthrallment, but Hannah didn't feel embarrassed, not even a little, as she nodded. The memories came sliding back quickly about what they'd done in the bunkroom. Her cheeks grew warm because she only had to think about Jude and her whole body heated up.

Vojalie laughed, a bright sound like bells chiming. "You don't need to say anything more. I can feel your experience. It glows from your entire being."

She didn't know about 'glow', but she definitely felt all fired up again.

"Hannah, this probably won't help at all, but you are the woman I would wish for Jude, warm and loving, very unselfish. But my opinions aside, what do you need from me?"

Hannah spoke from her heart. "Can this thing be undone? Do I have to be a blood rose?"

"I'm afraid that die is cast. Your issue now will be all about the mastyr with whom you bond."

Hannah sorted this through in her mind. "But if I don't bond with Jude or anyone else, I can keep my life as it is."

"Theoretically, but as you must already know, the blood rose drive is very powerful."

"Tell me about it."

Vojalie chuckled softly. "But let me ask you, when you've reflected on your life, and to me you seem like the kind of woman who would do that often, did anything in particular surface repeatedly as a desired hope or dream?"

Hannah thought back to the journaling she'd done over the years, even a few of the altered books she'd made pasting in all kinds of things into several old books. "I guess if there had to be a recurring theme it would be a desire to make a difference."

"And would being a blood rose make the kind of difference you envision?"

"In Jude's world, maybe. But I meant Port Townsend, my world, the human world. Not Kellcasse."

"But *your* world, the one you live in and delight in is at least half-realm. Just because the borders haven't changed, that doesn't mean Jude, his Guardsmen and many other realm-folk crossing the access point to Port Townsend haven't already altered the dynamic in *your* world."

"I suppose you could look at it that way. I just don't want this. The worst part is I'm told that other mastyrs will come after me if I don't bond with Jude, and I know that they're not all as wonderful as he is."

"My dear, can you hear what you just said?"

"You mean the 'wonderful' part."

"Yes, that bit."

"But why wouldn't I feel that way about Jude? I've known him all my life, and I trust and respect him. He's like family to me."

"Did you find it strange, then, to make love with him?"

The question was deeply personal, but again Hannah didn't mind. Aside from the fact that enthrallment was in play, she trusted Vojalie.

Still, the question forced Hannah to pause and to think. Had it bothered her to have sex with Jude?

She finally shook her head. "I was only troubled because he's realm, I'm human, and I've never seen myself going long-term with a realm-man. But no, it was easy to make love with him. I wasn't even nervous. The whole experience was amazing and charged with, I'm not sure how to say this, passion, I suppose."

"I can sense what your time with Jude meant to you, but I'm also sensing that you're unaware of the layers of your affection for the mastyr. So let me ask you this: if you'd had this kind of sexual encounter with a human male, what would you be thinking right now?"

Hannah blinked for a moment, her thoughts becoming perfectly clear. "I would start seeing him, I suppose, then see what happened next, see if we had something real, if we could blend our lives, if it could work."

Vojalie nodded and smiled. "And there you have it."

Hannah tilted her head. "Vojalie, it can't be that simple. I mean he's Jude, it's the whole blood rose thing, it's Margetta-the-freak."

At that, Vojalie laughed outright. "I have every reason to believe she would hate being spoken of like that."

Vojalie then settled her hand on Hannah's arm. "Try to shift out of the horror you're feeling and approach this situation as you would if you were dating a human. Be with Jude for a time. The bond is only completed when your mating frequencies engage and lock into place, and not a moment before. And that has to be a decision of the will; it can't be forced.

"If after a time, you find you can't tolerate either being with him or being a blood rose, we can address the issue together. For instance, we could devise a number of security measures to protect you from unwanted mastyr attention. How does that sound?"

Hannah breathed yet another sigh of relief. She'd felt so trapped, unable to see any kind of alternative. But these simple, very workable suggestions eased her. Maybe she was a blood rose, but it didn't mean that she had to commit body and soul to anyone unless she wanted to.

As her gaze drifted over the dark stretch of the Strait that led all kinds of ships and smaller craft into Puget Sound, she suddenly felt a sense of impending loss. Kellcasse was a beautiful realm full of canals, waterways, and small lakes all set in lush woodland.

But Port Townsend was her world, her life. How could she ever leave the Gold Rush to make a life with Jude on Castle Island? The whole prospect seemed impossible.

~ ~ ~

Jude had been to Hannah's home a few times before and liked the way she'd improved it over the years. The house was essentially a small cottage built on the hillside with a view to the open waters of what he knew to be Admiralty Inlet.

She'd opened up the walls that separated the living, dining and kitchen to create one larger space. Very nice. And she'd decorated with white, lots of black and dark grays then an occasional shot of pink. She had a piece of carved driftwood on the round, solid wood dining table, but other than that, and a couple of paintings of wooded beaches, she'd chosen against a typical maritime look and feel. No rope-bound tables, anchors, or seagulls in her place. Not even one seashell.

Her place was modern and charming.

Even so, his guard-size body seemed to take up too much space, and he thought it a fitting way to describe their present predicament. This vast wave had washed through both their lives, leaving her with unwanted powers, and building within him a lust for her hard to contain because she was a blood rose.

He'd been one hundred years without the influence of a woman in his life. How could he possibly embrace one now? Forget that he'd made a decision to keep away from long-term relationships. Just what kind of life could he even offer Hannah?

He had two jobs. He oversaw the day-to-day running of his realm, staying in touch during his waking daylight hours with all the various city and community leaders. And once full dark arrived, he patrolled with his Vampire Guard seven nights a week.

And Hannah had her bar.

None of this made sense to him. It would be one thing if his blood rose had been a realm-woman, who knew and understood everything about Kellcasse, his role, and who he was as a vampire. But Hannah owned a bar in Port Townsend and spent every waking minute there. Even on a simple, logical level, how would this even work?

When Davido moved onto the porch and waved for him to follow, Jude joined him willingly. He'd hoped to have a chance to talk privately with Davido and was grateful when Hannah had invited Vojalie to the roof deck.

Leaning on the porch railing, the troll smiled up at him, his blue eyes crinkling and the three rolls of his forehead lifting slightly. "So you are the latest mastyr to get struck by lightning, eh?"

Jude laughed. "Lightning. You've described it exactly right." He leaned his forearms on the railing as well and shifted his gaze out to sea. He liked Davido, one of the ugliest trolls in the Nine Realms. But he was ancient, wise, and had tremendous charisma. If he'd been a vampire, he would have been fierce. But his troll height, at least a foot shorter than Jude's, had forced him to carve out a different kind of life for himself, one that he wore with grace.

"I didn't know until I fed from Hannah, what was really going on. We'd had a mutual attraction for months, but each of us had kept the stops on. Then a wraith-pair showed up at dawn outside the Gold Rush and Hannah saved my life by burning the mated vampire."

"Sweet Goddess! You didn't mention this when we pathed together this morning. How did she burn him?"

"She's harnessed fire in a way I've never seen before."

"My wife will be well-pleased to learn of this. She said she was feverish until you called. Now I understand why."

Jude shifted slightly to face him. "What would you do in my shoes? I mean, if I leave her alone, another mastyr is bound to come after her. And the worst ones won't hesitate to abduct her."

Davido left the railing, pivoting toward Jude, as he rubbed his thumb in the valley between the top two ridges of his forehead. "Give her a helluva lot of security, and maybe stick close for the next few days. Nothing is settled until you forge a bond with her. I know this feels sudden, but it seems to me, with what you've just told me, that your relationship with Hannah has been building for a long time."

"I suppose if you look at it that way." The sound of laughter drew his attention inside the house. The women had descended, Vojalie elegant and remarkable in a flowing lavender and green casual gown and Hannah in her blue jeans and white shirt.

At least she was smiling, which was a good sign.

He couldn't help turning in her direction like a compass needle drawn to true north. From the time he could remember, he'd thought Hannah beautiful beyond words, especially close up. Her eyes were her best feature, then her full, high cheek-bones, her straight nose, her lips. Or maybe it was her expression, as though lit from within with the sheer joy of life.

"Try to think of it," Davido said quietly, "as a problem to be resolved, or even a string of small problems, rather than a massive disaster that needs to be torn asunder."

"It feels huge."

Davido laughed. "Love always does."

But before Jude could counter this completely inaccurate remark about 'love', Davido moved swiftly inside. He crossed to his wife and took her hand, kissing her fingers. The old troll seemed to be a great romantic at heart.

Jude remained by the doorway, watching but not listening. Hannah didn't know how well she fit into his world, or how comfortable she was with realm-folk. But then she'd been raised in the Gold Rush, and from the first day that the U.S. had opened up official relations with the Nine Realms, her father had welcomed Realm-folk into his bar. Jude had held Hannah when she was born and had seen her through every phase of her life.

But even from the first, she'd had a real love of life that he'd responded to. Maybe he'd even encouraged her, pushed her to go to college back east, to take a summer and tour Europe, even to spend a month on a sailing ship. He was sure in that time she'd meet a soul like her own and return to Port Townsend with a husband.

In the end, she'd come back engaged to Mark Jackson, a controlling asshole that had made Jude want to punch his lights out. Jude had never been happier when Hannah dumped his sorry ass. Sell the Gold Rush. What a douche!

Hannah's mother had died way too young, when Hannah was only seven. Jude had spent time with her then, as did many of the realm-folk, who saw her as orphaned, even though her father was a loving, involved parent.

The fact that she'd ended up with realm abilities seemed natural, since Kellcasse, by way of its people, had been such a huge part of her life all these years.

But how could they possibly make a life together? And maybe more importantly for the immediate future: How was he supposed to keep other mastyr vampires away from her?

Chapter Four

When Hannah bid Vojalie and Davido goodnight and watched them vanish, she put a hand to her forehead. She turned to Jude. "It's one thing to watch you fly, but they just disappeared."

"I know," he said, nodding. "That couple has a helluva lot of power."

"I'm so glad they came."

"It's a sound idea to have security for you. I should have thought of it myself, but I was too caught up in the situation to see clearly." He then told her that one of his lieutenants, Paul, and another powerful Guardsman, would serve as her bodyguards, whether here in her home or at the bar, or wherever she needed them to be. They had orders to contact Jude at the first sign of the approach of another mastyr vampire, or any other trouble.

Hannah felt tremendously relieved. She might even be able to relax a little. "Thanks for taking care of this."

He frowned. "I only wish I could stay with you, but I need to be out with my Vampire Guard. We still have unanswered questions about the recent massacre in the north, and I'll be heading out there later tonight to see for myself. Not to mention the two wraith-pairs that actually crossed the Sound earlier at dawn. I need to figure out what's going on, and the only way I can do that is in Kellcasse."

"You have to go, Jude. It's for the best on every front. I'm sure of that."

He drew close and took both her hands in his. "We'll figure this out for you, Hannah. I want you to be at ease and comfortable despite the changes you're going through."

"Vojalie gave me some hope. She said I'd always be a blood rose, and we could find ways to keep me safe from encroaching mastyr vampires."

"Absolutely. Like I said, we'll keep exploring options and create a security detail that will work for you." Jude's frown deepened. He'd never appeared so upset before.

"What's wrong?" Hannah felt his unease.

He shook his head. "I feel like somehow this is my fault. I mean, I'd been dogging your heels, anyway, making every excuse I could to be at the Gold Rush. And now you're a blood rose."

"You can't blame yourself. I felt the same way. Whatever this is, fundamentally we both felt the same way."

Even as Hannah said the words, she felt very strange, like she was in the supply closet all over again and Jude was there watching her. She took a deep breath, trying to settle the butterflies down, but once more her knees felt really weak.

For her — and this was the hardest part of all — she felt so much for Jude, longing to be with him, craving him.

He still held her hands, but he moved closer. "I just wanted to be near you." He then smiled. "And I'll never forget that moment, which now seems absurd. I mean, you had a bottle of ammonia in one hand and ugly yellow cleaning gloves in the other. It wasn't exactly a romantic place or time. I thought what harm could there be?"

At that, Hannah chuckled softly. "No, not romantic at all. Then everything changed."

"Hannah, I'm so sorry. If I could undo that moment, I would. I'd meant absolutely nothing by it."

"I know. I believe you."

When movement hit the corner of her eye, she yelped as two vampires landed on her porch. Jude even moved to position himself in front of her protectively. He relaxed immediately afterward, of course, when he saw who they were, then headed to the door.

She recognized them both as well. Paul was one of Jude's lieutenants and the other was one of his team leaders, Alex. Her heart warmed at the thought that Jude had sent two of his best men to guard her.

He glanced back at her. "Your detail has arrived."

She offered each a beer, but their refusal was firm; they were on duty. After Jude talked things over with his men, Paul and Alex took to the air to stay in flight above her house.

Jude returned to her. "You won't be seeing them, Hannah. They'll be in the air, patrolling your home the entire time. If anyone approaches, they'll hold them for questioning, then they'll call me. I'll return immediately to deal with the situation. Okay?"

"Of course."

"And when you're ready to head to the Gold Rush, or anywhere else, just contact Longeness, and he'll let either Paul or Alex know."

For the first time since Jude had pushed her to an awareness of what she'd become, she finally began to trust that things might just be okay. "That sounds good. And thank you so much for bringing Vojalie and Davido in. I adore them both, and Vojalie really did calm my nerves."

"Good, I'm glad." He nodded briskly, moving back to her, but his gaze suddenly caught and held in a way that stole her breath.

"What is it?" she asked.

"I'm remembering. And Hannah, for what it's worth, the time I spent with you in the bunkroom was one of the finest experiences of my life. I want you to know that."

Her chest rose and fell with each deep breath she took. "I feel the same way."

She leaned toward him with no particular intention in mind, but he must have read something deep in her soul because he quickly took her in his arms and kissed her.

Hannah held onto him, feeling sad and aroused all at the same time. The divide between them was so great, as big as the entire breadth of the Strait. Despite the changes she was undergoing, she was human and intent on living a human life and Jude was, well, Mastyr of Kellcasse Realm.

She gave herself to that kiss, however, feeling it could possibly be the last time she'd ever feel his lips on hers again or his powerful arms holding her tight.

He pulled back, but before she could say anything else, he strode to the open doorway, then launched into the air.

~ ~ ~

Jude headed to his house situated on Castle Island in the middle of Kellcasse Realm. The island was renamed in the last century to reflect the home his wife had built for them. Despite his sadness of losing his family, some of his best memories were inside the castle. Of being with Naomi, and of course, his daughter, Joy, who had been born there. The castle was always a welcome destination point.

He flew carefully, however, even a bit slower as he headed home, his gaze panning the horizon constantly for sign of the Invictus, or anything else out of the ordinary. He passed over a number of villages, many lit with candles and oil lamps, and a few with electricity.

He loved the variety of communities in his world, the trolls with their love of drinking and dancing, the howling shifters towns, the industry-oriented elven population and the magical, warm-hearted fae.

Because of the diverse population, he had strict codes of conduct between species to prevent racial slurs and prejudice, and a small squad of elves and trolls who kept the forest gremlins from pilfering their neighbors. It was as hard to get a forest gremlin to embrace honest labor as it was for a rock to pick up and move all by itself.

When he reached the largest lake of his realm, with Castle Island at the south end, his heart both warmed and ached. He'd built this home with Naomi when she was with child. He'd let her have her choice of architecture and didn't blink twice when she said she wanted a castle. 'After all, Mastyr Gerrod has a very large one and the structure I have envisioned will be quite small by comparison. But we will have a boat house.'

A couple of years later, his little girl, Joy, with curly blond hair, had run up and down the stairs of his home scaring the shit out of him since he was afraid she'd fall and tumble down those same stairs. That is, until he realized she'd been half-levitating the whole time. She'd had that much power even as a child.

After their deaths, he'd never brought a woman again into this house. He'd never wanted to.

Until now.

And that thought also scared the shit out of him. He shouldn't be wanting Hannah anywhere near his home or in his life, for her safety alone. He wanted every Invictus in his realm dead, before he married again.

But for the first time since having taken that vow, his longings rose like a sudden flash-flood within his chest.

He tried not to think the thought, but the truth was that he'd give just about anything to have Hannah making a life with him in his home.

As he touched down in the stone courtyard, he heard a troll singing what he knew to be a beer-drinking song. Nothing had felt as normal as hearing Nathan sing. Not liking the word 'butler', he'd assigned himself a new title: Executive Castle Coordinator, or ECC, and was proud of it.

Jude didn't care what he was called; he loved having Nathan keeping his life working day and night.

He opened the large wood front door and passed through.

"Is that you, Jude?"

"It sure is. Am I smelling coffee?"

He moved past a large living room built with a couple stories high ceiling, inset with wood beams. Three tall, arched, diamond-paned windows ran along the east wall, flanked with sun-blocking shutters.

A long dining room came next, with tall, tapestried chairs, and a runner crocheted by his nanny two-hundred years ago. Naomi had loved the runner, so he'd kept it on the heavy, dark wood table all these years. A very large window made of the same diamond panes as the ones in the living room, framed a view of the lake. Across the water, a dozen villages climbed into the surrounding hills.

His own vision saw everything in a glow of green hills and blue lake.

It was a beautiful vista that one day he'd love for Hannah to see. Maybe if he shared with her some of the favorite parts of his realm, she might be inclined –

But there he stopped his thoughts cold.

What was he thinking?

He needed to guard against any such hopes or fantasies. Hannah loved her bar and belonged there. And he never wanted her to sacrifice what meant so much to her just because she was now a blood rose.

And he needed to stay focused on the Invictus and finding a way to run the last one to earth.

He passed through the hall that housed storerooms on the left and a butler's pantry on the right. Once a year, he brought in his lieutenants and lead Guardsmen, serving them a feast he catered from one of the talented, local elven restaurants.

Once in the kitchen, Nathan held up a tray of intricately decorated cupcakes.

Jude's brows rose. "Don't tell me these are from — ?"

"Yep. *Just Two Sweet* in Merhaine. Arrived an hour ago. Abigail sent them over. Actually, Elena did." His eyes glazed over for a moment. Nathan had a thing for Abigail's business partner and spent as many long weekends as he could courting the elven beauty.

"Well, this is a treat."

Nathan had a few crumbs clinging to the corner of his mouth. Trolls loved sweets.

Jude moved to sit at the large island. Nathan poured him a cup and slid a plate over to him. The cupcake was decorated with the front image of his castle. Jude smiled as he bit down.

Needing to bring the kitchen up to date, Jude had given Nathan full control over the remodel. The results were stunning. The entire layout was made of white marble and stainless steel and made for a serious cook, which Nathan was.

The kitchen had a north view of the lake and its rolling hills. Several villages could be seen in the distance, with cottages and shops climbing in various places all the way to the top. The most expensive dwellings sat on the ridgeline and had excellent views of Kellcasse in both directions.

As mastyr homes went, the castle was fairly small with an upper story of three bedrooms and his own large suite. Nathan lived in a detached guest house, the one connected to Naomi's boathouse and dock. Sailing had been one of his wife's favorite pastimes and she'd spent a lot of time on the water with Joy.

Well-groomed gardens, now in early summer's full bloom, pressed up against all the stone walls of the castle and more than one lattice-work took purple clematis as far as it would go. Naomi had laid out the gardens herself.

She and Joy were buried where they'd been struck down in the middle of the small peach orchard on the western side of the property.

Jude went there often to sit and think.

He'd once thought to build workers' cottages near the orchard, but Nathan, who had been with him from a year before his marriage, insisted on hiring outside help and services.

When he'd purchased the island, he'd built a stone bridge for all the non-flight laborers to use during construction.

As he sipped his coffee and took his time with the cupcake, he stared out across the lake.

He almost felt at ease, until Nathan started moving slowly toward the window, frowning. "What is it, Nathan?"

With a large pot he'd just cleaned still in hand, Nathan peered out the window. "Ordinarily, I'd say that's lake mist, but I swear I've never seen it look like that before. It's moving in a strange pattern."

Jude set his coffee down and moved in the direction of the door leading to the porch. This side of the island fell away, so that the gardens below had a terraced look. The porch itself he always referred to as a balcony, even though it was on the ground floor.

He moved to the center of the stone balustrade and stared hard. Using his realm cell-phone, he contacted his other lieutenant, Reese. "Do you have anyone near Castle Island?"

"You got Invictus sign?"

"No. I've got some kind of weird-ass mist on the lake moving steadily in my direction. Should hit in about two minutes."

"Rising from the lake?"

"No, moving across it like a thin strange fog. I don't like it."

"What do you need me to do?"

Jude felt sick inside his body the closer the mist drew. "I want you to keep all your forces away from this mist. It doesn't feel right to me. Bring a squad over here but do not engage. Just stick close enough to keep your eye on things."

"Got it."

The mist was maybe thirty yards away and closing faster than he'd thought.

Nathan, pot in hand, moved up next to Jude. "Is it me, or does it have a sickly sweet smell?"

"It does. Something like death."

And before Jude understood anything, Nathan dropped unconscious to the balcony floor, the pot clattering on the stone.

He made a quick decision and contacted Paul.

"Yes, Mastyr."

"I need Hannah at the castle, the back balcony and I need her now. This is an emergency. There's some kind of mist. But don't ... go past ... "

Confusion hit first, then he felt himself falling.

~ ~ ~

Hannah sat on the bench at the end of her bed, lacing up her soft, black leather work shoes when Paul about gave her a heart attack. He suddenly appeared on the porch outside her bedroom door and rapped hard on the glass.

Thank God she already had her jeans and tank top on. She was almost ready to head down the hill to the Gold Rush, but thought that on the way she might just give Paul a lecture about how *not* to go about scaring humans.

"Give me a sec," she called out.

She'd grabbed her cellphone, shoving it into her pocket, then started across the room.

Paul called to her. "Hannah, it's Jude. He's in trouble. He wants you at Castle Island. Now."

What surprised Hannah the most wasn't the announcement of trouble, but her instincts. She didn't think twice. She simply yanked the door open, shut it quickly behind her, then opened her arms to Paul. He pulled her hard against his side, then launched into the air and flew at top speed toward the realm access point, adjusting arms and feet while traveling.

"How long will it take?"

"I'm fast, but I can't do it in under three minutes."

The Kellcasse point was in the direction of Whidbey Island. But because Paul was realm, a tunnel in the midst of clouds appeared that led all the way down to the water.

A tour boat emerged carrying a variety of realm folk over to Port Townsend for the night, mostly trolls and a few shifters. Paul moved fast, speeding over the central canal that led into the myriad waterways that made up the island world of Kellcasse.

She might have enjoyed the trip, but the closer they got to Jude's home, she could feel him as though he was trapped somewhere and couldn't get out.

"Paul, what did he say?"

"He said it was an emergency and that he needed you and that there was some kind of mist."

"Mist?"

"That's what he said. Then nothing."

"What do you mean, 'nothing'?"

"I don't know. The call ended, but it felt like he lost consciousness."

"Go faster."

Hannah's palms were already tingling and her skin had started heating up. She warned Paul that she had a fire-gift power emerging, using Vojalie's description. Since she was pressed up against him, he was going to feel it. "I just hope I don't burn you."

"Don't you worry about that."

Another hill and another and another. More canals below, villages, boats, lots of boats and in the lanes, people on bicycles.

It was such a picturesque realm.

Then there were the Invictus.

Oh, God.

One more rise into the air to clear a hill and Kellcasse's large central lake came into view, with lights from scattered villages all around the perimeter glowing in the water.

Toward the nearer, south end, she saw what had to be Castle Island except that it was enveloped in a mist. And as Paul descended she could smell that it had a strange sickly odor.

"Drop me down at the end of the bridge and don't go near the mist. But you'd better get some of your Guardsmen over here."

"They're on the way."

As soon as he released her, she knew the heat she was releasing had given him some blisters. But she couldn't worry about that.

Paul called out. "He's on the balcony off the kitchen at the back of the house."

She ran into the mist, past the stone arch of the courtyard. She raced toward the wood door and flung it open.

She saw a golden light out on the lake moving closer.

Margetta.

No, no, no.

Lorelei had told Hannah all about the ancient fae and her golden light.

Hannah ran as fast as she could through the living room, down the hall, and found the door on the right that led to the balcony.

The golden light loomed now.

She saw Jude and reached him just as Margetta appeared through the mist, her hand extended toward him.

Death was in that hand.

Hannah let her power rise and as it did she directed her palms toward Margetta and watched flames leave her arms and hands, catching Margetta in the chest.

The ancient fae, also part wraith, shrieked in the horrible way the Invictus wraith had the night before, her pain obvious. She rose in the air, higher and higher and the mist flowed with her.

Hannah moved away from Jude and the troll who'd fallen near him.

She had one goal right now, not to make this easy for the woman who'd caused so much suffering in the Nine Realms and who had apparently been a heartbeat away from killing Jude.

She lifted both her arms and the tingling in her palms turned to fire once more. She aimed at the mist, wanting every last bit of it gone.

Margetta flew faster but everywhere the fire touched the mist, the mist evaporated.

She kept it up until Margetta's golden light disappeared and all the mist was gone.

When Hannah lowered her arms, her heart was racing so fast that she had to struggle to catch her breath. She forced herself to calm down, but all the adrenaline she'd released at finding Jude close to annihilation, had left her shaking.

She pressed her body up against the balustrade for support.

"Hannah?"

"Jude." She moved back to him, suddenly afraid Margetta had wounded him.

He sat up, looking dazed. "You made it."

"Just in time, thank God."

"Was it Margetta?"

"Yes, but she's gone now, the mist with her."

His gaze shifted to the troll. "Nathan, you okay?"

Hannah glanced behind her and saw that the troll now sat against the low stone wall, but his eyes rolled in his head.

"I don't think he can talk, yet, but he doesn't look injured or anything."

Movement in the sky had Hannah ready to fire up again, but she immediately recognized Paul, and worked once more at calming down. Paul dropped down to the balcony close to Nathan.

"What happened here?" Paul asked.

Jude shook his head, still sitting. "The mist came on so fast, then I just fell and blacked out. It happened in an instant." He turned to Hannah. "Are you okay?"

Hannah nodded.

Paul drew next to Jude, frowning heavily. "This has to explain the attack in the north, how those families died. The ancient fae must have used this mist to immobilize them, then killed them."

"I'd have to agree."

Paul extended his hand down to Jude, lifting him to his feet. Jude shifted on his feet, then planted a hand on the railing to keep his balance. "By all the elf lords, I'm still damn dizzy."

Hannah moved close and settled her hand on his arm, but it was Paul who spoke. "Mastyr, Hannah defeated Margetta. She even wounded her." He touched his own wrists and hands, patting them, trying to explain. "She released fire, Mastyr. From here, like this." He swept his arms back-and-forth in the air. "Fire."

"Sweet Goddess." Jude turned toward Hannah and took her gently by the shoulders, looking her over. "You're flushed again. Did you really do this?"

She nodded.

"Are you sure you didn't get hurt? You're shaking."

"No, not hurt. Adrenaline."

"Right." Then to Nathan, "How you doin'?"

"F-i-ne." the word came out slurred as he struggled to his feet. Picking up his pot, he shuffled in the direction of the back door. Hannah could see that the mist had really taken the troll down, another reason to believe that Paul was right, that Margetta had used the mist to kill the two troll families on North Island.

To Paul, Jude said, "I'll want all the team leaders here as soon as possible. Reese should be here by now. Tell him what you saw and have his team guard the castle for now. I doubt the ancient fae will come back tonight if she's been wounded, but I want to be careful."

Paul got on his com at once, talking to Longeness at the Kellcasse Communication Center, and delivered Jude's orders."

Jude slid his arm around Hannah's shoulders, then guided her toward the door. "Let's get you inside."

Hannah was happy to leave the balcony. "Good idea. I just wish I could stop shaking."

"You will. Give it time."

Once inside, Hannah saw that Nathan was sitting on the window seat with his pot in his lap. "I think your troll could use some rest."

"Good idea." He called out to Nathan. "Why don't you head to the boathouse and get some sleep." When Paul appeared, saying that the team leaders were headed in, Jude swept a hand in Nathan's direction. "Paul, can you see that he gets back to the guest house?"

"Of course."

Paul moved to the much shorter troll, and offered a foot.

"Oh, hell yeah," Nathan murmured. He set the pot on the table, then hopped on. When Paul had a tight arm around Nathan's shoulders, he levitated slowly to the door, then flew into the air, crossing over the balcony and heading toward the boat house.

Jude guided her to the kitchen island and had her sit down. "I'm going to fix some tea. How does that sound?"

"Really good. Thanks."

She perched on a stool as Jude opened a box and pulled out a couple of tea bags.

"Can you tell me exactly what happened?" he asked. "What you saw and experienced?"

Hannah understood. Jude now had his realm-ruler hat on. He needed to start figuring this out, then to take what precautions he could on behalf of his people and his Vampire Guard.

She spared no detail.

~ ~ ~

When Hannah finished her recounting, Jude filled the tea-kettle with water and set it on the cooktop to boil. He offered her a cupcake, but she shook her head.

Jude had never, not once in his long-lived life, faced a situation in which the enemy had employed something akin to a nerve gas.

Nathan had fallen quickly to the effects of the sickly-sweet scent, and he hadn't been far behind.

He tried to recall what he'd experienced, but it all seemed vague and he still felt slightly disoriented.

So the ancient fae had a new weapon in her arsenal.

Great.

He agreed with both Hannah and Paul that Margetta must have tried out her mist first on the troll families at North Island and now here, hoping no doubt to make a quick kill, then move in on his realm.

And the only reason she'd failed was because of Hannah.

Sweet Goddess.

Moving about the kitchen eased him. He needed to be doing. Hannah now sat on the stool at the island, her hands clasped together on the marble. She no longer shook, but she had grown very quiet.

"You know what's funny?" she said at last.

He brought two cups down from the shelf and planted them next to the cooktop, adding a tea bag to each. "What's that?"

"That once Paul told me you needed help, I didn't think twice. I could feel your desperation. How is that possible?"

He shook his head, checking to see if the water was boiling yet. Not quite. "I honestly don't know."

"I'm guessing it's connected to my being a blood rose. Maybe even because I've donated."

He met her gaze and thought her expression might be accusing. Instead, she just looked confused.

And beautiful.

He didn't say anything, but waited beside the tea kettle, checking until finally the water started to boil. He poured the hot water slowly over both tea bags.

Bringing the cups with him, he rounded the island and sat on the stool next to Hannah. The flush on her skin had dimmed, leaving her with a really healthy glow. "So, how the hell do I thank you for this, since you just saved my life and Nathan's?"

She'd already started lifting the bag up and down when she turned to him, a half-smile on her lips. "There's no need for thanks. I'm just so grateful that Paul got me here in time."

He'd almost bought it. That's the tape that kept running through his head.

She carefully draped the tea bag over the side of the cup and stared at her hands. "And I really can't believe that I did what I did? I had fire coming out of my hands and my arms. At least my palms are no longer tingling."

"By the way, how long had your hands been bothering you like that? I can recall you mentioning it a couple of times over the past few weeks."

She chuckled softly. "Can't you guess how long?"

"Since the closet?"

"Yeah. Since then."

"Well, I suppose it makes sense."

She took a sip of her tea. "I should have known something was going on, but I ignored it. I guess I just didn't want to see that there was anything more to my interest in you than just this." Her gaze encompassed his body.

He smiled. Once again she'd offered him an ego-boosting moment.

He searched her beautiful violet eyes. He tried to think back to the moment he'd become entranced by them, and realized it might have been well before the supply-closet incident. "Hannah, I'm just now remembering something that happened about a year ago, and which I think first set me down this path with you. Do you recall the time that a couple of human males were harassing an elven woman about her body, asking her terrible questions?"

"Oh, I remember that, and it was well over a year ago. I don't think I've ever been so angry."

"You threw them out. Well, you didn't, but Hector did, on your orders." Hector was her well-muscled bouncer who performed his duties extremely well.

Hannah scowled. "Both those idiots were drunk, but they had no right to ask about her pointed ears and her sexuality. It was completely degrading."

"Yes, it was. But you stood up for my people and that's when things started to shift for me. I saw you as more than the little girl I'd known. I finally saw that you'd become a woman."

He held her gaze and all his cooling-down desire for her, suddenly heated up once more.

"Jude," she whispered. Her cheeks turned a rosy color once more, but this time not because of her fiery power but because he sat next to her.

He drew in a deep breath. This wasn't the time to be sexing her up. He had men flying in. "How's the tea?"

She nodded. "Good. I like the cinnamon flavor."

He drank from his mug. "Hmm, needs something." He left his stool and headed back into the kitchen, "Want honey with that? Because I do."

He hadn't realized what he'd said until suddenly her perfume, a scent that he now understood was part of her blood rose-ness, permeated the air." He turned to her and saw that though she'd brought the cup to her lips, she wasn't drinking.

'Honey' conjured up all kinds of things and she'd apparently started conjuring.

He closed his eyes, drinking in the smell of her with heavy drags through his nostrils. She tasted like that as well, like the seashore and roses, and he wanted more of that flavor in his mouth.

Ah, hell.

He left his tea on the sink and moved in behind her. He stroked her arms up and down, then leaned close and nuzzled her neck. *I want your honey. Will you give me your honey again?*

He felt a shiver pass through her and she slowly turned her head so that her lips were now inches away.

When her lips parted, he closed the distance and kissed her. And not a simple kiss, but deep and probing.

She responded, moaning softly. *I keep thinking about the bunkroom.*

Me, too. He drove his tongue in and out. *I want to do that to you again.*

I'd love it if you did.

He drew back and looked into her eyes. "It will complicate everything. I mean, the first time, in the bunkroom, we were both caught up. But if we sleep together now, after we both know what's going on, I don't think it will be simple."

She caressed his face. "Right now, nothing is simple, but the moment that Paul came in, telling me that you needed me, I guess I knew then that whatever this is, what it will become, can't be denied. I feel so much for you and not just sexually. The way I felt coming here was as though some part of me had already planted roots in Kellcasse. But please remember that I've built a life in Port Townsend, and I mean to keep that life."

"Hannah, I would never want you to do anything else. I know what the bar means to you, even the communication center. And I would hate to have what's happening here take you away from what is most important to you."

She kissed him, once, warmly, then held his gaze. "And I do understand your commitment to ridding the world of the Invictus. I'm with you one-hundred percent. Please know that. I value more than I can ever express what you and your Guardsmen do." She nodded briskly several times in a row.

His heart was on fire. He pulled her swiftly from the stool, gathered her up in his arms and kissed her again. From deep within his body, he felt his mating vibration thrum to life, wanting to connect with Hannah, wanting to make her his forever.

She drew back, her eyes glistening with desire. "What is it that I'm feeling?"

He told her.

Her eyes went wide. "Really? Your mating vibration? But that's rare, isn't it?"

"It is for me." He drew her close again and just held her. He knew they would make love again soon and he wanted to be with her, to be connected to her in that way, so badly, he ached.

"I've turned this situation over and over in my head and I know it's asking a lot, but Hannah I really think we should stick close together, at least for the next few days."

"That's my thought as well. If Margetta attacked you again and I couldn't get to you—" She broke off, clearly unwilling to say the rest.

He nodded. "So we're agreed?"

"Absolutely."

He stayed with her like that for several minutes, just holding her, rubbing his hand along her waist and up her back, letting her feel his gratitude.

He only released her when the first of his men arrived on the balcony. "And my men are here."

She pulled her cell from the pocket of her jeans. "And I'd better contact the Gold Rush."

~ ~ ~

Hannah called the bar and spoke to Amelia, her right arm, letting her know she wouldn't be in for the night. If Amelia sounded astonished, why wouldn't she be? Hannah never took a night off, or rarely, and even then just for a couple of hours.

She explained that she was helping the Mastyr of Kellcasse at his Castle Island home - difficulties with his communication center - and that she needed to stick close to him for now. Not quite the truth, but she didn't like the idea of telling any of her staff that she could now shoot fire from her hands.

Despite that, Amelia drove way to close to the truth when she teased, "Geez, Hannah, sounds like you're a blood rose."

Hannah swallowed hard, then covered with, "As if." She had no interest in broadcasting her own personal difficulties right now.

Amelia giggled. "Well, enjoy your time with the mastyr, but if I were you, I'd ask to see his bedroom." She then laughed again and Hannah ended the conversation with her own forced laughter, asking to be transferred to the communication center.

After asking Sandy to call in a couple of people to fill in for Hannah's slots, she could finally be at ease. This wasn't exactly how she'd expected her night to go.

When she slid her phone back into her pocket, movement on the balcony drew her eyes once more.

The Guardsmen, who served as team leaders had started arriving.

Hannah realized she knew every one of them by name and it pleased her when each greeted her like an old friend. Yet somehow it didn't surprise her that Jude never moved more than an arm's length away from her.

When the last arrived, and Paul drew up the rear as he herded everyone into the living room, Jude held back. Once out of earshot, he turned to Hannah. "Did you have to touch at least half of them?"

Hannah had never been so surprised. "I like touching. And I only held back with the hugs because I could feel you bristling beside me."

"Damn right I was bristling."

But Hannah only laughed and kissed him on the mouth. "It's nice to know I'm not the only one suffering here."

"That's not exactly the reaction I was looking for. I don't like you touching other men."

She wanted to chuckle again, but she could see that he was serious. And whatever weird realm creature she was becoming, she could tell that to keep laughing wouldn't just wound his pride but would make him distrust her.

She recalled all the chatter on the loop about this one aspect of being a blood rose, that the men who bonded with their women, became rather ferocious in their territorial marking rites.

Something inside her went weak just thinking about it. She drew close and grabbed his woven shirt with both fists, pulling him down to her. But she wouldn't let him kiss her. Instead, she whispered, "Any way you can mark me, vampire, so that other men will stay away?"

She wasn't sure exactly what kind of response she'd been looking for, but he suddenly picked her up in his arms and flew her outside, onto the balcony, to a portion of the wall that would hide them from anyone inside.

He pressed her up against the stone and ground his hips into her. She felt his arousal and her legs lost function all over again.

He spoke hoarsely into her ear. "I'm going to mark you again and again, do you hear me? I'm going to fill you up so that no male, human or realm, will dare to touch you. Does that answer your question?"

He kissed her hard, so that her entire body just about melted into the stone behind her. What Jude could do to her with just a few words, the wonderful mass of his muscular frame, and his warm, moist lips.

She had that eternal sensation again of wanting to stay with Jude just like this, never moving, just being with him and feeling him, and having desire move like fire through her veins, forever.

Finally, he drew back, breathing hard. He held her gaze. "Part of me wants to apologize, but to hell with that. We're in this, and you need to know everything, especially what it's like for me."

She grabbed his shirt again. "Jude, let's make a pact right now not to apologize for anything that relates to this blood rose madness, okay? I know I'll want to as well, but I think it'll just make things more difficult."

He nodded. "Agreed." Slowly, he shifted his hips away from her, but stayed close. "And I need to calm down."

At that, she smiled again. "What? You don't want to face your men like this?"

She reached low and ran her hand the entire length of his arousal.

He arched and hissed. "Oh, Sweet Goddess, Hannah."

She planted her hands on his face and kissed him with more affection than passion. "Do you know how many times I imagined kissing you just like that?" She couldn't help but smile.

"No. How many?"

"About a thousand."

"Is that all?" His turn to smile.

"Okay, I'm going inside. I need to freshen up a little, but I'll join you for the meeting."

"Good. I want you there."

She didn't try to prolong the moment. Instead, she located the downstairs bathroom and splashed water on her face. She stayed put, giving herself a little alone time to collect herself.

Ten minutes later, she heard Jude's deep voice coming from the front living room and headed in his direction. She caught the décor along the way, as well as the style of the architecture and knew instinctively that a woman's hand had been involved.

Probably his wife's, the woman he'd lost all those decades ago.

As she entered the living room, she stayed near the entrance to the dining room. Seeing a dozen heavily muscled Guardsmen in one room was an overwhelming experience. Each ranged in height from six-three to six-six and wore what she considered to be their supremely sexy black leather-based uniform.

If the ceiling hadn't been as high as it was, the room would have felt claustrophobic.

Jude relayed all that he knew about the mist, the sickly-sweet scent, the effects on him and also on Nathan, and his belief that Margetta had used the mist to kill the troll families in the north.

What he didn't know was whether her wraith-pairs were immune or not. And if they were, the entire realm faced a crisis of enormous proportions.

"But how can we find any of this out?" Paul asked.

"I hate to say this, but only experience will give us the information we need. There's just no other way. We don't know where Margetta lives to try to spy on her."

Hannah added her thoughts. "I get the sense that Margetta is just trying out what might be a new ability for her. If Jude and I make ourselves visible throughout the rest of the night, and the Guardsmen were spread out hunting for mist-sign, we could be anywhere at a moment's notice."

All eyes turned toward her, and she felt a warmth spread over her cheeks. For a moment, she wished she'd kept her mouth shut.

But Paul said, "That's actually a very good idea. Better to have some control by hunting, rather than to wait for another slaughter."

Jude met her gaze and she felt him press against her mind telepathically. *Hannah, I don't want you in the line of fire.*

But Jude, I already am and Paul's right. Better to have some control in the situation.

Jude nodded, then addressed his men. "As you can imagine, I'm concerned for Hannah's safety."

"Everyone here is," one of the Guardsmen spoke up.

"Here, here," went around the men.

She knew these men and which ones had wives and families and what each laid down every night to battle the enemy. "I feel the same way about all of you. I hope you know that."

Another said, "We do, Hannah. That's why you find a couple of us passed out in your bunkroom every night at dawn."

Laughter erupted this time and she joined them.

But when her gaze landed once more on Jude, she saw a look in his eye, of deep appreciation, that pierced her heart. She felt two things at once: The huge divide that separated them because the focus of each of their lives was so different and her ever-present affection for him.

She had to look away, to remember that she'd made a promise never to allow what was important to her to be set aside for the needs of a man. Maybe Jude wasn't Mark Jackson, her ex. And yes, Mark was a real dick for demanding that she sell the bar to basically prove she loved him. But the situation had the same difficult resonance – what she'd have to give up and what Jude wouldn't.

So she calmed herself down, wanting desperately to keep her perspective as the hours and possibly days wore on.

Jude brought the subject back to the point. "Here's the way this needs to go. I want every Guardsman on patrol. And Paul, bring in everyone on leave. You're to give this basic information to each of the men, about the mist, about Hannah, but that we need to draw Margetta out. One of my fears is that she'll use some of our people again to try out her mist-making ability and more innocent realm-folk will die. So, let's keep a sharp eye out for the mist. Heavy patrolling everywhere." Which covered a lot of miles. But Jude's Vampire Guard was three-hundred strong so no one balked at the order.

"And Reese, I know the shifters aren't fully ready, but let's put them on the ground. I'm thinking about that scent, it was sweet but in a way that smelled decayed. Maybe a shifter will have a better chance at locating the next intrusion."

"I think that's a great idea. They're chomping at the bit to see some action."

"Then tonight would be a good place to start. Go ahead and contact Rayle. I'll leave you in charge of that part of the operation. Just get them out there." Rayle was the alpha and had command of his men.

Reese took off.

They also discussed whether or not to alert the general population to the mist problem. The central issue became clear, that to let all of Kellcasse know about the killing mist could cause wide-spread panic. And if that happened, Jude would end up with more problems than his limited Guardsman force could possibly manage.

And never mind about the bad press Jude would receive in the Kellcasse Chronicle. He'd be crucified in print. One way or the other, this was shaping up to be a PR nightmare if he and his Guard didn't figure out how to deal with the killing mist.

Hannah made her own contributions, her observations of the mist, of Margetta, how the ancient fae seemed able to pull the mist with her, and that Hannah's fire dispelled it.

In the end, it was agreed that each of the team leaders would alert their men about the mist and the necessity of avoiding it, but to report any sign to Longeness and his staff at the Kellcasse Communication Center. Longeness had the ability to reach the Guardsmen all at the same time when needed.

As the Guardsmen dispersed, leaving by the front door this time, Hannah hurried with them for the simple reason that she loved to see vampires in flight, especially the super-fit Guardsmen.

Jude stood close to her, one arm around her waist.

As the last one left, he turned to her and said quietly, "I don't like you looking at other men, either."

"I wasn't eyeing them as 'men'. I was watching your Guardsmen fly. It's an impressive sight."

He growled softly and nuzzled her neck, nipping her throat. She gasped, since the possessive gesture lit her up.

But she pushed away from him. "Don't start that or we'll never leave this place."

Jude remained where he was but she could see that he was using every ounce of his energy to retain control.

"Fine," he said at last. "Then let's fly."

Chapter Five

Jude realized that taking Hannah into the air had one solid advantage: Her body was pressed up against his and he could keep her there. She slung an arm around his neck for balance, adding to the closeness. And for one of the few times in his life, he cursed the leather Guardsman coat he wore because it prevented him from feeling the swell of her breasts against his side.

If all went well, he'd have her back at Castle Island in a few hours, safe and sound.

Then he'd have her in his bed.

What are you thinking about, Jude, because the air has this wonderful spicy, peppery scent.

He chuckled. *Nothing much. You. My bed.*

She sighed. *How long until dawn?*

Too long.

But as they cleared the hills to the east and continued on a slow path in that direction, he decided he'd better get with it. He touched the com at his shoulder and contacted his communication center. "How we doin', Longeness?"

"I've been collecting data from the time that Paul gave me your orders. So far, my staff says ninety-five percent of your Vampire Guard is in the air. And with the exception of one, whose wife is in labor, the remainder will be airborne within the next half hour."

"Excellent. Any reports of mist?"

"Nothing yet."

"I want to hear about even the smallest hint of trouble. Are you monitoring the civic forces?" Each county had a policing force that worked within county lines and Longeness could listen for reports of mist from their centers as well. In an emergency, Jude could command all the county teams.

"Yes, Mastyr."

"Good. Again, let me know if anything even slightly off-center shows up, no matter which part of the realm."

"Understood."

Jude signed off and flew Hannah in an easterly direction. She was very quiet, yet he felt her intensity. "Are you comfortable?"

"Yes, thank you. But please don't worry about me. I don't need small talk, not at a time like this."

"You must have read my mind."

"Well," she said, "I have known you a long time, that even in social situations you're not given to trivia and useless chatter."

"I guess you do know me." He was smiling as he passed over a village built up along both sides of a canal. He heard troll laughter, a baby crying in the distance, a dog barking.

As he flew above a nearby woodland, he dropped lower to the earth and saw three shifters racing at top speed, going almost as fast as he could fly through the trails below. Reese had done a good job getting them in the field.

He felt himself relax just a little. He had every part of his realm covered right now; vampires flying back-and-forth, looking for Invictus or mist sign, shifters on the ground.

He flew Hannah over his land, talking to her quietly, naming the villages and towns, the creeks, canals, streams and lakes.

When he reached Kelltah Bridge, he hovered above it for a moment so that she could take it in.

"What a beautiful bridge." She leaned forward to get a better view, holding his neck tightly.

"The bridge connects two distinct communities."

"And I think this is one of your larger canals."

"It is." After a moment, he put them back in motion, passing over another mile or so of rolling hills and woodland. Again, he saw a squad of four shifters, in wolf form, racing along one of the ridgelines.

"They're beautiful when they're running. Elegant."

He would never have described a rough shifter as elegant in either wolf or realm form, but seeing them through Hannah's eyes he knew what she meant. "Shifters pride themselves even more than Guardsmen do on their athletic conditioning."

Another village and waterway, arched with three bridges. Another woodland.

When Hannah stiffened, then gasped, he immediately drew them to a halt, hovering in the air. "What is it, Hannah? Do you see mist?"

"Oh, God, I'm so sorry. No, nothing like that."

Jude looked around carefully, searching for mist despite her assurance otherwise. "Okay, so what caught your attention? Had to be something."

"Jude, again, I apologize. It's just that I suddenly realized that I can see really well and it's nighttime."

He worked to settle his heart down and to not yell at her because he could sense her remorse.

He put them in flight again. "That's part of your power base, to see well at night."

"I might not be happy about the blood rose thing and this fire-power I have, but I'm loving being able to see everything as though the woods are glowing."

He turned north, wanting her to see one of their prettiest villages with a predominantly hard-working elven population. Many were expert stone-masons and it showed.

He told her what he was doing and wasn't surprised that when the village came into view, she made many cooing sounds of appreciation. "It looks like a village in Britain. I swear every window has a window box jammed with flowers and trailing vines. And look at the flower baskets hanging from the lampposts."

"I thought you'd like it."

As he drew close to the center of the village, she asked, "What's going on there? Look at all the lights strung everywhere. Is it a wedding? Oh, my God it is! A real elven wedding. Would it be rude to draw close enough to see their arms joined with a vine?"

Both the elven and fae communities made use of vines during the ceremonies, wrapped around both husband and wife's forearms, to symbolize their bond.

He flew as near to the square as he dared, not wanting anyone to see them, then hung in the shadows for Hannah to get a good look. He wouldn't disrupt the ceremony for anything.

Switching to telepathy, he pathed, *Can you see their arms?*

I can. It's so beautiful and look, she's very pregnant.

It's a tradition among many of the elven, the fae as well, and a sign of prosperity, for the woman to be with child on the day of her nuptials.

Well, I think it's lovely. Even magical.

But she stiffened once more in his arms. At first he didn't know why until she said, *Jude, I'm frightened. I can sense that Margetta is nearby. She's very close.*

You're sure? He rose steadily into the air, higher and higher and got Longeness on the com. Just as he was about to talk to him, Jude saw a line of mist on the nearby canal that sent a chill through his heart. "Longeness, I have mist-sign. I need as many Guardsmen as possible surrounding the elven town of Chelana. Tell them to avoid the town center. There's a wedding in progress."

"Got it. I have four within a five minute arrival time and another … let's see, seven, no eight at the ten minute mark."

"Thanks, just send them to me."

To Hannah, he said quietly, "Back-up's on the way."

"Okay." Her arm tightened around his neck.

He felt her distress and slowed his flight, moving steadily in the direction of the mist. "Hannah, how did you know she was there?"

"It's weird, but I felt her presence. I can still feel it."

"Has to be your fire-gift."

The next moment, mist appeared at the railing of the nearby canal. It began pouring over the pavers of the road and moving swiftly toward the square.

"Jude, what are we going to do?"

"I don't know. If I approach the mist, I'll pass out."

The moment the mist reached ten feet from the nearest realm-folk, no matter the species, each simply slumped to the ground. The process looked like dominos falling.

Jude had never felt so helpless to intervene, and he really hated that feeling.

~ ~ ~

Hannah knew that she could make a difference, because she'd already confronted Margetta once. But she didn't see the woman anywhere, and she was afraid to start working her fire-gift without at least knowing the woman's location. "Rise higher in the air, Jude. I need to look down on the crowd. My God, how fast the mist takes them over. It's like watching a flood and being unable to help anyone."

The moment Jude had lifted them another fifty yards in the air so that she had a bird's eye view of the square, she groaned. "I can see Margetta now. She's right next to the bride." The mist reached the lovely red-haired woman in white lace, and she dropped along with her attached groom onto the pavers at Margetta's feet. The bride fell on her side, her free arm surrounding her swollen belly protectively.

The crowd had grown very quiet as more and more people fell unconscious. Those opposite the fallen, stared in mute confusion as the mist rolled toward them and a slight murmur of concern went up until the mist reached them.

By the time another minute had passed, the entire square had fallen silent, at least two-hundred vulnerable realm-folk awaiting slaughter.

Margetta lifted her gaze upward and called out, "Come to me, Hannah. We need to reach an understanding."

Jude spoke into his com. “Longeness, let the incoming Guardsmen know that Margetta is in the Chelana town square. Make sure they remain at two-hundred-yards distant. Looks like we’ll be negotiating. But keep them flying. I’ll want the troops here in case the Invictus show up ready to do Margetta’s bidding. So far, no one else is here to support the ancient fae.”

“Understood, Mastyr.”

Something flashed in Margetta’s hand as she knelt beside the bride. “Fly me closer, Jude. Oh, God, Margetta is holding a dagger to the bride’s throat. Do you see it?”

“Yes, I do.”

“Why is Margetta doing this?”

“Testing the field. She wants to know how powerful you are as well as the limitation of her mist. The only good news is that it looks to me as though her mist also affects her own army of wraith-pairs, otherwise they’d be present right now, awaiting her orders.”

“Just get me as close as you can without being affected by the mist.”

“Come to me, Hannah, or the bride dies.” Margetta pulled the woman’s upper body onto her lap, exposing her pale throat. The bride’s crown of lavender flowers slid off her veil and onto her husband’s arm.

Margetta made a surface cut, so that a small rivulet of blood slid down the side of the woman’s neck.

Hannah gasped. “I have to go to her.”

“No, Hannah.”

She turned to look at Jude. *Just keep your telepathic frequency open. We’ll talk the whole time. But I can’t let her die and neither can you. We'll have to wing it, but I know we can figure something out. I also know that I can't have this woman's death on my conscience.*

Jude's nostrils flared and he pressed his lips tight together. *I understand.*

He set her down outside the circle of mist that lay like a soft veil over the prone realm-folk.

That smell is horrible. She stepped off his boot. *Just talk to me.*

Jude backed up swiftly, positioning himself thirty feet away, out of range of the mist, but he stayed on the ground. *The mist appears to have strict limitations, but I can still smell it even from this position.*

Hannah didn't glance in his direction, but stepped carefully over several people, working not to crush hands or limbs.

As she approached Margetta, she thought yet again that even though the woman personified evil, she was beautiful with even features, a straight nose, and violet eyes not unlike her own.

Margetta's eyes, however, turned silver in that moment, which Hannah knew meant she was attempting to employ her enthrallment skills.

In response, the fire element of Hannah's strange emerging power began to burn hot. Her skin grew flushed, and she lifted her chin. She released a sudden burst of that hot energy directly at Margetta's mind. The ancient fae winced, but her eyes returned to normal.

"So, you've got some power." She looked Hannah up and down. "Yet, I don't understand what you are."

Hannah's gaze slid to the blood still trickling from the elven bride's throat and to the shiny silver blade in Margetta's hand.

Meeting Margetta's gaze once more, she responded, "I have no idea, either. Nor does Vojalie, except that I'm meant to create balance in the Nine Realms."

"Balance?" Margetta laughed. "Don't be stupid. Now here is how this is going to go. You've got a very simple choice: Either come with me right now, or the bride and everyone in this lovely community square dies. What shall it be?" She rolled the blade at the woman's neck, creating a second surface slice, but with a stronger flow this time.

Jude, did you hear Margetta?

I did. You're not to leave with her. She has only one intention; she will kill you.

I know. The problem is, I know the bride. I didn't recognize her because we were so far away, but a year ago she and her boyfriend came into the Gold Rush and announced their engagement. She started to tremble. *Can you tell me something?*

Anything.

How fast can you really fly?

What are you thinking?

Hannah worked to keep her heart steady. *Only that when I'm airborne and high enough, I'll blast her, but that means I'll probably fall and someone will need to catch me. Sound okay to you?*

Hannah, you could die. You don't know all the power she has. And what if I can't reach you in time?

Then I'll die doing something worthwhile. She'd made up her mind that the last thing she could ever allow was this woman to die on the happiest day of her life.

She stepped forward and held her arms out to the ancient fae. "I'll go with you."

The woman smiled and moved the bride to rest on the pavers. Blood still flowed from her neck.

Margetta leaped toward Hannah in a swift upward flight, faster than Hannah thought she could move. In a split second, she caught Hannah beneath her arms and lifted her into the night sky. She was moving incredibly fast, ever higher. The sickly sweet smell came off the ancient fae's skin so that it was all Hannah could do not to throw up.

She watched the world grow smaller and knew the time had come. She reached deep within herself and found the vibrating source of her fire and began in slow stages to build it until Margetta was pressing her hands tight to Hannah's ribs.

"You really wouldn't be that stupid to risk your life when we're almost at five thousand feet. Because if you burn me again, I'll have to drop you. Silly girl." She increased the pressure.

Hannah had already made up her mind and didn't hesitate. She let the fire-gift within her explode outward.

Margetta screamed as she released her, a scream that turned into a witch's cackle. "It's a long way down, my dear. I don't suppose you can fly, can you?"

The force of the separation, as well as Hannah's growing power, held her in a brief spurt of levitation. "Go to hell and by the way, you're not all that!" She then drew on her power once more and sent fire from her palms and arms that blasted the ancient fae, thrusting her backward at least forty feet.

Margetta flew shrieking toward the northeast, a ball of fire. Hannah knew Margetta would survive. She had no illusions about that. Only something more profound than blistered skin would take the ancient fae out.

But the bitch would need time to recover.

However, now she was a mile above Kellcasse, and her levitation began to slip. She tried to recapture it, but failed, and she began to fall, gathering speed way too fast.

Hannah tilted backward so that she had on odd view of a very pretty night sky above her. *Jude, I'm earthbound. Catch me if you can.*

She hoped to hell that Jude was somewhere close, but if not, then she was satisfied that she'd done what was right and her conscience was clear. She'd gotten Margetta away from a lovely bride and groom and all the guests and had hurt her enough to eliminate her as a threat for the rest of the night.

She held herself in a cradled position, hoping against hope that Jude would see her and catch her.

~ ~ ~

When Margetta had plucked Hannah from the square and lifted her straight into the air, Jude had reacted instinctively, racing toward the spot where she'd been.

Though most of the mist had retreated with Margetta's flight, some remained and he'd had a hard time remaining conscious.

But Hannah's voice in his head forced him to look up. When he saw her plummeting toward the earth, he got his ass in gear, forged his way out of the remaining mist, then shot forward barely three feet above the terrain hoping like hell he could intercept her.

He was barely going to make it and tried to gain as much altitude as possible. Unfortunately, he was only twenty feet above the ground when he caught Hannah in his arms, her own force-of-fall driving him hard into several tough cabbages.

It hurt.

He lay very still, afraid to discover his back had been broken or that just catching Hannah had somehow injured her. He took a breath then another.

"Am I alive?" Hearing Hannah's voice caused him to heave a deep sigh of relief.

"Yes, you are, thank the Goddess. Are you injured?"

"I don't think so, but are you? I mean I was traveling fast and you had no room to give."

"I'm pretty strong, if bruised."

Hannah struggled to right herself, then gained her feet.

Jude stared up at the stars for a moment. He watched as several of his Guardsmen began to gather in the air, looking down at him.

He ached in a few places, especially where the row of cabbages had broken his fall. He lifted his head. Not bad. Then his shoulders. Ouch.

Hannah extended her hand to him. It was so odd that she would offer to help him up, he and his two-eighty frame. He took her hand, but instead of standing up, he pulled her onto his lap and did a limb-by-limb search to make sure she really was all right.

"I'm okay. I am. You caught me."

She rested her arms on his shoulders until he was satisfied that she was uninjured. He slid his arms around her waist and kissed her once. "Thank the Goddess. I saw a streak of flames so I take it you let loose with your fire-power."

"I warmed it up, then I let her have it. I don't think she thought I would risk falling. Of course, I'd rather be dead than held captive by her. Besides, I knew I had a pretty good shot at you catching me."

"Except like an idiot I raced into the mist when she took off with you and got dragged into a serious bout of confusion."

"You did not! What a rookie move and what were you thinking?"

"*Reacting* is the word you're looking for. I tried to launch after you both, but that damn mist is fast-working and powerful. Fortunately, she took most of the mist with her, but it still took me a minute to recover."

His lieutenant, Paul, drew close, hovering a few feet away. "Mastyr, everything okay over here?"

"We're good. What's going on in the square? Any sign the bitch has returned?"

"None, but I wasn't far when I saw Hannah and Margetta explode into a blaze of light. I've never seen anything like it."

"Is that what we did?" Hannah asked, looking up at Paul.

"It lit up the entire countryside and she was still burning when she took off. I don't think we'll see her for the rest of the night. But we'll stay on patrol."

Jude, still holding Hannah in his arms, rose to his feet. She slid her arm around his neck. *Can we really go home for the night? I'm about done in.*

Me, too.

To Paul, he said, "Contact Longeness and let all our troops, shifters included, know what's going on. But I want everyone patrolling until dawn. As for the wedding at Chelana, I want a medical team over there to make sure everyone is all right. You'll take care of things for me?"

"Absolutely. But what do I tell the wedding party and their guests? How much info do I share?"

Jude had been debating this from the first, just how much to let his people know. He understood full-well there would likely be a media backlash against him because of what had happened here tonight. And it would make splashy headlines: 'Bride Faces Death on Her Special Day'.

He made his decision. "I'll bring in Frida and her team of PR specialists and let them decide what to do. In the meantime, just let everyone know that help is on the way."

He got Longeness back on the com and ordered him to send his PR team over to Chelana. "I won't be able to answer any questions tonight, but I will tomorrow. In the meantime, have them try to keep the Kellcasse Chronicle from going overboard in its write up."

"Done. But just so you know, I alerted Frida the moment you mentioned Margetta was at a wedding."

"Thank you for the foresight. I owe you one for thinking ahead."

"You're welcome, Mastyr."

With that, Jude launched into the air, holding Hannah tight once more. She trembled now, not surprisingly.

"You smell like cabbages, Jude. You'll have to have your coat and leathers cleaned after this."

He smiled that of all the things she could have said to him, even that she could have railed at him about dragging her into this mess and risking her life, she talked about getting cabbage stains off his leathers.

He nuzzled her neck, even while flying. "And you smell like fire with just a hint of roses and the seashore underneath."

She laughed but hugged him tighter still.

He flew her back to Castle Island, cradling her in his arms. She shook, but he understood the cause. Battle could do that to anyone, not to mention a mile-long flight straight down.

Dawn was hours away yet, but he refused to put Hannah in jeopardy one more time. He'd take her back to the Castle and spend the rest of the night with her there. Hopefully, the day as well. She'd been through a lot and needed her rest.

While in flight, he contacted Reese, requesting a squad to patrol the Castle Lake just in case Margetta made a way-too-speedy recovery. He doubted she'd be back tonight, but he wasn't taking any chances.

Once daylight came, Margetta as predominantly fae, would need to seek shelter as well, so he felt fairly confident that he wouldn't have to worry about her killing mist until the following night.

Jude, though I don't like to mention it, I sure hope your fridge is stocked because I'm starving.

Me, too. And don't worry. Nathan always keeps the shelves packed. I'm sure we'll find something to satisfy.

Her hand found his chest and she rubbed in a gentle motion. *Oh, I'm absolutely certain we will.*

He didn't even try to misunderstand her, but put on a little more speed. A meal. A shower. And Hannah in his bed.

He felt lightheaded as he descended onto the back balcony, landing easily just outside the door. When he set her on her feet and led her across the threshold, he could see that her body was still flushed from battling with her fire-gift.

Once inside, she turned toward him. "Jude, I know this may not seem like a big thing, but is there any way I can get some of my things over here? I need my brush, a change of clothes, other stuff."

"Don't worry about it for a second." He used his cell this time to contact Longeness, then handed it to her, saying, "You ask for everything you want. I have a large staff who can get whatever you need within the hour."

She took the phone with a hearty 'thank you', then drifted into the hallway to make her request.

Part of Jude wanted only one thing, to hustle Hannah upstairs to his bedroom, feed from her vein and make love to her. But what he wanted right now didn't matter. Hannah was starved and he'd make sure she had a good meal before he did anything else.

He headed for the fridge, and pulling it open, found a tureen of fresh beef and noodle soup. His stomach growled, making him aware that the last thing he'd eaten hours ago, was a cupcake.

He toasted some French bread, poured out two glasses of sweet German wine and by the time Hannah returned, he was ladling out two bowls.

"That smells wonderful."

He gestured to the table by the bay windows. "Have a seat."

"Thank you for this." She held a hand to her stomach as she sat down in one of the chairs so that she could look outside. "How close to dawn are we?"

"A few hours yet." He didn't even have to think. He had an internal clock, as all sun-sensitive realm-folk did. He could have stated the time to the minute, if he'd wanted to.

He brought everything over in quick trips, then sat down beside her. She picked up her spoon, dipped, sipped and moaned. He loved that sound, no matter when she made it. "Jude, this is freaking amazing. I've never cared for soup much, but I think I'm in heaven."

"Nathan studied in Paris for a year."

"Seriously?"

"He made quite the stir. I think he became a minor celebrity for a time. But damn he can cook."

"He sure can. The bread is perfect. All of this. Thank you."

He met and held her gaze for a moment. "You did great tonight."

She drew in a quick breath. "I've never been so scared." She sank her spoon again and this time maneuvered a thick noodle into her mouth, though her fingers shook. *Adrenaline,* She pathed.

I know. Been there.

Despite the fact that he normally didn't care for small talk, he decided to do it anyway for Hannah's sake. He knew how hard it was to come down after a battle. He gestured to the lake and named the various villages in the distance that rimmed the shoreline. A second glass of wine helped, and she finally stopped shaking.

She even smiled.

"What?"

"I was told by a very wise woman, to ask you an important question."

"And who is this woman? Do I know her?"

"Amelia, my manager."

He choked on his wine. Then swallowed and wiped the corners of his mouth. "Amelia, the wise? The one with purple stripes in her hair who has dated at least a dozen bikers and one ex-con?"

"Just because she has a thing for bad boys doesn't make her unwise. But I'll let you judge for yourself the wisdom of her advice. She told me that I should ask you to show me your bedroom."

Jude's nostrils flared, and his heart expanded about twice its size. At the same time, his leathers shrunk. "I take it back. Amelia is brilliant."

He didn't act on what he felt, however, even though all he wanted to do was haul her into his arms and get on with things.

Instead, he sat with her at the table striving for patience, especially given that another kind of hunger had risen; he needed to feed. But Hannah needed her things before they retired.

Movement out on the lake showed that his Guardsman were already on patrol.

After sufficient time had passed, he rose as he spoke and started gathering up the dishes. He rinsed and left things in the sink. He wasn't about to do a full clean-up when Hannah was there, waiting.

She rose as well, and at the same time, his phone rang. After shutting off the water and drying his hands on a towel, he answered. "Yes, Longeness."

"Mary is at the front door to the castle with Hannah's belongings."

"Thanks. The timing is perfect. Much appreciated. You're off in a few?"

"Ten minutes."

"Say hello to your wife."

"And take care of our girl." Longeness and his wife had often gone to the Gold Rush, until she'd discovered she was pregnant with twins. They'd stuck close to Kellcasse since.

"I will." Everyone loved Hannah.

He put his phone away and waved Hannah toward the front door. "Your things have arrived."

"That was the phone call?"

"Yep. Standing orders. I want to know who's coming to my house before I open that door."

"Makes total sense."

A vampire named Mary brought a rolling flight bag full of Hannah's clothes. She was beautiful, with straight black hair and large blue eyes, and had often spent time at the Gold Rush. She'd been married to a Guardsman years ago, but he'd fallen to an Invictus attack.

After the two women exchanged a few laughing comments about digging around in other people's closets, Mary wished them a blessed night. Jude offered the same farewell, and a moment later, she took off into the night.

He watching Hannah staring after Mary, clearly amazed at the way vampires could travel so easily in levitated flight.

Jude took the suitcase in hand, then guided Hannah to the stone staircase at the left.

"This really is a castle, isn't it?"

"It is. It was my wife's dream and though I might have chosen something different for myself, all I cared about was making her happy."

He heard Hannah catch her breath. "Oh, Jude. She should have lived. Your daughter, too. I'm so sorry."

"I couldn't agree more but it was a long time ago."

She stopped him just at the bottom of the stairs, tugging on the inside of his elbow. "I can feel your sadness, though. I've always felt it, and if I could erase it, nothing would make me happier."

Jude stared down at her, hardly knowing how to respond. He knew she'd spoken from her heart and maybe that's what troubled him. Hannah was such a good, worthy woman. "You have a very tender heart, Hannah. I mean, I know you've cared for my men and even for me with all that you do for us in your bar. But I don't think until this moment, I ever realized that everything you do comes from that tenderness."

She looked taken aback. "Thank you. I'll always remember that you've said that to me." She then took his hand and started up the stairs.

Jude felt gut-shot in a way he couldn't explain. He didn't even know why he'd told her about Naomi's love of this house, but he was so at ease with Hannah. Of course he always had been. He'd just never thought it would lead to this, to Hannah in his home, leading him upstairs, to his bedroom.

Sweet Goddess.

His heart ached, not just because he missed his wife and always would, but because Hannah was … well, exactly who she was and he loved her for that, more than he'd ever understood before.

He tried not to think about it, however, nor did he have to make any decisions right now, but the transformation of his relationship with Hannah seemed to be moving at light speed. But to what possible end when Hannah wanted to sustain her life in Port Townsend more than anything else in the world and he ruled an entire realm?

~ ~ ~

Hannah took a long, cool shower, grateful that she had her things with her. Mary had been thorough, even adding a few things she hadn't put on the list, like two more pairs of shoes and socks. She'd delivered the requested nightgown as well, just not the one Hannah had asked for.

She had at least a dozen nightgowns ranging from long flannel to the lavender silky one now hanging on the back of Jude's bathroom door.

Mary had chosen a very skimpy negligee, made of sheer lavender fabric trimmed with lace. She'd never even worn it before, but had been saving it up for something special.

And now Jude would see it.

When she had her hair washed, she finally left the very large, Jude-sized shower with massaging jets and a variety of heads aimed at all angles. She blew her hair dry, loving the texture after having used Jude's crème rinse.

She'd have to find out where he got it because it was fabulous. With all his hair, of course, he'd need to work hard to keep it under control.

Once her hair was dry, she slipped into the nightie.

But as she looked at herself in the mirror, without a single light burning, her skin had a warm glow that had never been there before. Even her features seemed stronger somehow, though not in a bad way.

Closing her eyes, she opened up to what resided inside her now, to the heat always close to the surface, to her tingling palms, and to the ability to fight off the most powerful fae in the Nine Realms.

She felt the vibration of it and began to explore. The Nine Realms was a world of vibrations, something she'd always known but now experienced. Jude had used physical vibrations when they'd made love in the bunkroom and just thinking about them again loosened the tendons at the backs of her knees. He also had a battle vibration and maybe that's what this resonance of heat was within her body as well, a tool of war.

She opened her eyes, but still didn't see reflected a warrior like Jude and his Vampire Guard. She was just a regular sort of person who owned a bar in one of the best places in the U.S.

And she was a blood rose.

She took another moment to sort through her new inner life and found the vibration attached to the other part of who she was in the realm world. Closing her eyes once more, she took a moment to examine the blood rose vibration and felt more than anything that it had a nurturing quality, which made sense since it was designed by the hidden mysteries of this world to feed a mastyr vampire. She still couldn't believe that her blood could relieve Jude forever of his chronic blood starvation.

As she connected with this frequency, it led her straight to Jude who she had heard earlier moving around in his bedroom. Opening up to him, she could feel the level of his hunger in the same way she'd been starved when she sat down to have her beef and noodle soup. Jude needed her blood. Badly.

She could also tell that he'd held back letting her know of his hunger, something she valued so much about him. He seemed to always be thinking of others.

The errant thought ran through her head: *So just how far have I already fallen in love with Jude?*

A shiver ran through her at the thought of donating again, of giving up the most important element of her body, the thing that nourished every living cell. She would give this up to Jude, and do it happily because Jude was … well, Jude.

She'd never thought in a million years that she'd have a sexual relationship with him, but here she was, just a few feet away from his bedroom.

She opened the door slowly to catch a glimpse of him before he saw her. Having already showered in another room, he sat on the end of the bed in nothing but a light blue towel, his head bent over as he carefully worked a brush through his damp hair.

The bedroom also had stone walls like the outside of the castle, heavily mortared, very masculine and beautiful. This room fit Jude extremely well. But she also saw the feminine hand of the designer since the room was decorated in shades of blue with floral drapes reminiscent of at least a century past.

Another tall, arched, diamond-paned window filled the entire north wall, giving an almost cathedral-like impression. The ceiling, with a dozen exposed dark beams, slanted at an angle at least eight feet above the tops of the heavy wood bedposts.

She felt overwhelmed because within the walls of this chamber lay Jude's history, the marriage to his Naomi, the birth of his daughter, Joy, whom he'd cherished, and the life the couple had been in the process of creating for themselves.

"I feel honored to be here." She spoke quietly, her voice almost hushed, as she moved into the room.

Jude lifted his head, craning his neck to see her. He didn't say anything right away, but his gaze slowly went down her body, dwelling for a moment on the sheer fabric over her breasts then taking his time to have a long look at her legs. His spicy, peppery scent rolled through the air, which drew her toward him.

He was so gorgeous with his black curly hair, an exotic, animal-like mane around his shoulders and down his back.

Stay put, she pathed. *I just want to take a moment.*

He nodded slowly, setting his brush on the bed next to him.

How far they'd come, she thought, in just a couple of days, from her efforts to ignore him in the doorway of the Gold Rush Communication Center to this moment, seeing him seated, wearing only a towel on the end of his bed.

She knew he'd never brought another woman here, not in all these decades. One more reason why her time with him right now felt important, even sacred. She still had the conviction that it was temporary, so she wanted to make the most of every moment.

"So you feel honored?" he asked, his gray eyes questioning.

She nodded, moving close to him now. The bed was built up high so that his long legs were at an easy angle to the floor. She put her hands on his knees and slowly pushed them apart, moving between. The light blue towel split at the same time, so she decided to hurry it along, pulling each side to fall on the bed next to him and exposing him.

He was in a beautiful, aroused state, the size and strength of his cock a perfect representation of who he was. She leaned her hips into him so that she could feel him against her body while she took his long, thick hair in both hands, entwining her fingers. "I thought a lot about doing this, about getting so tangled up that I could never get free."

His hands slid beneath the negligee, landing on her waist, kneading gently. "And I've pictured you here in my bedroom."

"I wanted to be here." The thought flitted through her mind that these circumstances, that she was a blood rose and carried within her an anti-mist weapon, might have been the only way she could have landed here with Jude. Was it a miracle or some kind or a curse?

Right now, though, she didn't care. She was here. Jude was here. Nothing more needed to be said.

He dipped his head to her cleavage and ran his tongue the length. She shivered, tugging on his hair, leaning close to smell his spicy scent.

She realized she'd always loved the way he'd smelled. Only now, it was all mixed up with his maleness and her need for him. He lifted up and kissed her, surrounding her with his arms, pulling her close.

Deepening the kiss, he plunged his tongue inside, which took her breath away. His cock moved against her abdomen at the same time, hunting to be inside her. His hips arched and she felt the length of him glide up her stomach then back down.

He was just so much man to savor, touch, caress. She carefully unwrapped her fingers and slid her hands beneath his still-damp hair. His muscles rippled beneath her touch as she traveled down the center of his back, leaning over his shoulder to reach his waist.

Then her hands journeyed north again, feeling the width of his back all the way to his massive shoulders.

Pushing his hair down his back, she fondled his left shoulder, rubbing her fingers along the dips and swells, following with her tongue and her lips, licking and kissing.

She loved that he responded by nuzzling her neck and pulling her closer, pressing his hips into her again and again.

"Jude, may I do something to you?"

He drew back, smiling at her. It amazed her that a man who could look so ferocious just by frowning, could appear incredibly tender with just a smile. "Anything you want, Hannah. And I do mean anything."

"Good." Her cheeks warmed, because this was all so new and she was demanding things. "Why don't you peel back the comforter all the way to the floor, then stretch out on your stomach."

"My stomach?" His lips twisted. "You sure that's what you want?" He let her feel him again, as he curled his hips.

"I won't deny that you tempt me, but I'd like to indulge in another of my fantasies."

He groaned softly, leaned close and nipped her throat, then moved around the foot of the bed to strip away the unnecessary bedding.

When he was face down, spread eagle, she sighed with great contentment. She drew near his feet, stroking his thick calf muscles, then climbing up on her knees between his legs. She took turns with each leg, kissing and licking, steadily moving up until she could stroke his sack and his buttocks at the same time, then added more kissing and licking. His occasional groans and the flex of his hips told her she was on the right track.

Jude had muscles everywhere so that even his buttocks were tight, worthy of tongue worship. She spent several minutes fondling and licking all over his bottom.

She parted his almost waist-long hair, and worked her way up his back, massaging at times, fondling, kissing and licking. She wanted to remember Jude stretched out like this, letting her enjoy his body, for as long as she lived. Especially, since she had no confidence that they really could build a life together. Their lives were too disparate.

She stretched out on top of him, her legs on his, her toes reaching a little lower than mid-calf. "Spread out your arms."

He obeyed quickly and she did the same, so that her arms were on top of his. She drew in a deep breath, wondering why this felt so good.

"What made you think of this?" he asked.

Hannah chuckled. "I love how you look. Even before I developed a serious desire for you, I used to watch you play darts just to enjoy how you moved. And once, when you were a little drunk, you picked Paul up, who is a big man, and spun him on your shoulders. You have such athletic grace. And now I'm feeling all that muscle beneath my body. It just makes me happy, like I'm balanced on top of a raft, heading out to sea."

His turn to laugh. "A raft, huh?"

"Sure, why not." She wasn't certain if she'd ever been so content in her life as she was now. "But I have a question for you, Jude. What's your pleasure? What would you like from me? Did you have certain fantasies that played over and over in your head, I mean besides the ones you mentioned when we were together last?"

Chapter Six

Jude decided he'd died and gone to heaven. For a woman to ask what his pleasure was, pleased him not just sexually but deep within his masculine soul.

Of course, the last thing he'd expected was for Hannah to spread out on top of him, and he sort of thought the 'raft' thing fit. He loved the idea of moving through heavy seas together, joined like this.

Mostly, he loved that she took so much pleasure in his body. He worked out and he battled the Invictus almost nightly, so yeah, he was fit. But experiencing her appreciation made the hours he put in all the more worthwhile.

As for his fantasies, she'd already fulfilled one just by walking into his bedroom and wearing a very short nightie, which was sheer enough that he could see her breasts and her beaded nipples.

She still wore the nightie. So yeah, there was at least one thing he wanted to do to her while she had it on.

"I want you on your back."

She slid off him quickly, maybe as anxious as he was to move things along. When she was lying beside him, he took his time and caressed her face, then kissed her, loving that her hand caught his arm and she dug her nails in a little.

He slid his hand lower to first stroke her throat where he intended to bite her later, then lower to caress her breast. "I love this," he murmured, running his hand over the sheer fabric.

"I'm glad, but you'll have to thank Mary. I asked for a nightgown, thinking about one of my long comfortable flannels and this was what she packed."

He chuckled. "Mary deserves a raise."

Hannah smiled her lovely smile. "Yeah, she does."

He kissed her again, then shifted to look down at her. Sweet Goddess, she was beautiful and her violet eyes glowed. The air had become perfumed with her roses-and-seashore scent.

He moved lower and kissed her throat licking several times, teasing her vein then descending to her cleavage where he set up shop. He loved Hannah's breasts and as he kissed her, he pathed, *This was a fantasy, taking time with you like this, exploring.*

"It feels so good."

He shifted just a little, and through the very thin fabric, he flicked her nipple with his tongue until it puckered for him, then he settled in for a suck.

Working her breast, he forced it into a mound so that he could devour, taking as much as he could into his mouth, stroking and suckling at the same time. That Hannah made cooing and moaning sounds, caused his hips to flex. He wanted to take care of her in every way possible right now, to pleasure her, to take her to the pinnacle, repeatedly.

He decided to start right now. Pivoting slightly, he moved his body off to the side of hers. Using his free hand, he massaged her between her legs, feeling her wetness, which again had his cock begging for mercy.

But he wanted to take his time.

While he continued to suckle her breast, he pathed, *Spread your legs for me.*

She moaned again and her hips dipped into the mattress as she let her legs fall wide. "Jude. Oh, God Jude. You're barely touching me and I'm so close."

He wanted to help that along right away, and sent a gentle vibration through his fingers.

She cried out, her body arching. "Jude!"

He eased two fingers inside, moving slowly, but he increased the vibration, loving that he could do this for her. Her hips reacted by rocking in a steady motion, and her hands dove into his hair. He suckled her faster so that she cried out repeatedly.

He moved his hand in quick thrusts, driving in and out of her well.

She panted now, her body in a state of beautiful tension.

I'm going to take you over the top now.

"Yes," she breathed. "Please."

He increased both the vibration and the speed of each thrust of his fingers, and just like that, she cried out long and loud, her well pulsing, her breaths like puffs, her body writhing. *Jude ... so wonderful ... can hardly breathe ... and it keeps coming.*

He sustained all that he was doing, savoring her hands pushing and plucking at his head almost at the same time, until at last she eased back down.

He let his fingers rest inside her and hc released her breast. Her nipples were in stiff peaks now, and he kissed each one, loving that she'd orgasmed and that he'd done that for her.

His motivation of course could never be pure since each climax would flavor her blood, and he wanted to taste her pleasure each time he sucked her vein. His cock twitched at the thought.

When he removed his fingers, he stretched out beside her and kissed her, nibbling on her lower lip, and working her mouth once more with his tongue. He loved making love to her.

After a moment, she said, “Do you know what I’d love to do?”

“What?” He stroked her cheek with his thumb, then kissed her again on the lips.

“I want to feast on you Jude, and I want to feel your vibration in my mouth.”

His whole body arched hard at the thought, and he groaned with the thought of her mouth on his cock.

She smiled, leaning up to kiss him. “I take that as a ‘yes’?”

“Unh-huh,” was all he could manage.

She took her time though, and made him suffer, because when she sat up on her knees, she lifted the lace hem of the nightie and slowly drew it up and over her head. His eyes feasted, then his hands, because he couldn’t keep from touching her. He was so ready that he almost pushed her onto her back and climbed between her legs.

But she caught his right shoulder and held him back. “I want to do this first.” Her violet eyes glittered.

He nodded, incapable of speech.

As he spread his legs, she moved her knees between then lay down so that part of her legs dangled off the bed. Her hands worked his thighs as she dipped and nibbled his sac.

His hips arched when she moved to the base of his stalk. He gripped the sheet in both hands, his hips now pulsing as she kissed, nipped, and sucked her way up his cock.

The anticipation of her warm, wet mouth, had his cock jerking with need. She lifted up and rimmed his crown first with her tongue, which sent a groan past his lips again.

She didn't suck right away, instead she plucked at him with her lips, then swept her tongue over him. She even got him wet then blew on him until he was mad with desire.

When she finally took him in her mouth fully and began to suck, a series of heavy grunts left his mouth. "Hannah, that's amazing. I love that you're doing this to me."

But after a moment, something changed that increased the heavenly sensation. He felt warmer. Was she adding her fire-gift? "Are you doing that?"

She pathed, *I may not have your ability with vibration, but I thought you might enjoy a little heat. Do you?*

He released a heavier groan in response. His lips parted and his breathing grew ragged.

Can I feel your vibration now?

He obliged her, releasing a gentler version for her mouth.

That's fantastic, She pathed.

But as her sucking grew warm and more rapid, coupled with the vibration that had his cock in an uproar, he grabbed her shoulders and cried out, "Stop."

She chuckled as she shifted position, planting her hands on either side of his waist. "How did you like the heat?"

"Unh," came out as another eloquent expression.

"Now let me tell you what I need."

She wrapped a hand gently around his hard cock. "This … between my legs … now."

~ ~ ~

Hannah hadn't expected Jude to move as fast as he did, but he was half-levitating as he rose up and flipped her onto his back.

She landed with a thud that made her laugh. He kissed her, his tongue driving deep as she spread her legs for him. He maneuvered his hips, using his hand to position his cock at her entrance. The vampire was so not messing around.

The moment she felt him, she cried out, even though he was still kissing her. He didn't stop, either, when he began to push. Instead, he took her tongue between his lips and suckled, a sensation that had her crying out all over again. When he added a vibration, she once more whimpered.

Jude, what you do to me.

He began to push inside, slowly at first then faster, adding another vibration down low. Hannah felt as though she'd moved into some kind of alternate universe, drifting along, not quite herself, yet experiencing every sensation sharper than before.

She reached deep within and found the frequency connected to her fire-gift. She began slowly within her well and warmed everything up.

Oh, Sweet Goddess, Hannah. You don't know what that feels like. He thrust deeper in response.

She could feel ecstasy building between them like a vibrating inferno of sensation. She also knew that his mating frequency had come to life as well, something that touched her abdomen, reaching inside for a matching vibration.

Then she felt it, her own mating vibration, one more indication she was becoming realm.

Hannah, do you feel that?

Yes, it's amazing. Touch me with your mating frequency. Please. I want it.

First, I need to bite you.

She cried out and shifted her head to the side. While he continued to thrust into her well, he swept her hair away from her throat, then licked her in long sweeps until her vein rose.

He made chuffing sounds deep in his throat, a reminder that he was vampire and not human, something she'd grown to love so much.

As he angled his head, she focused all her attention on the bite. When it came, a jolt of pleasure dove straight through her well and she almost climaxed.

But she wanted to hold back. There would be a moment when they could come together and share ecstasy as one, and that's what she wanted, almost as though it was life to her and nothing less.

When he formed a seal with his lips and began to drink, he slowed his hips which helped her to calm down. She caught the nape of his neck and fondled him. With her free hand she once more, and with tremendous pleasure, slid beneath his hair and explored the rise and fall of his shoulders, his arms, his back, his buttocks.

He groaned now as he drank her down, as he took her life force within. His body grew warmer to the touch as well, and his muscles seemed to expand, both a result of her blood and the expression of her fire-gift.

When he released a stronger vibration through his cock, she began to pant, both holding her release at bay, yet bidding it to come forward at the same time.

His hips began long, deep thrusts and her breathing grew more erratic, shallow and intense.

Finally, he let go of her neck and rose up on his forearms to look at her. "We're going to come together, Hannah, you and me."

She nodded.

And at that moment, his mating vibration began to stroke her own, so that her entire body felt engaged in the act. She could almost feel Jude's pleasure as he drove his cock in and out.

He began to move faster and whispered, "I'm ready."

She nodded once more, and as he increased his speed and the vibration deep within, ecstasy came as an enormous wave. It caught her up with an intense streak of pleasure that kept pulsing, then soaring up through her abdomen, up and up, so that she was crying out. When it all hit her heart, the orgasm exploded wide open, breaching the veil between the realm world and the heavens so that some part of her consciousness shot through the night skies.

But Jude's roar of ecstasy brought her back to his gray eyes and just like that she could feel his pleasure, how his seed ignited a thousand sensations and sent him into a profound release.

He roared again and again and before it was all done, she felt her body respond once more, until she was shouting against his roars and pleasure flew over every sensitive nerve. His mating vibration tightened around hers so that ecstasy flowed through every part of her body.

It took at least a full minute before each of the sensations began to pass, before her body would settle down, before Jude's cries and grunts started to ease back, before he could release his hold on her mating vibration.

All retreated in stages until she lay sweating, hot, and more satisfied than she'd ever felt possible.

"You're flushed. Are you okay?"

"I'm still floating around Jupiter, I think. You?"

"I have a buzz from that release. Hannah, it's never been like this."

"For me, either."

All talking ceased and eventually her breathing evened out, as well as his.

He lay on top of her for a long time, supporting himself on his forearms, yet still connected. He laid gentle kisses now and then on her throat, her cheeks, even her shoulders. When she started to doze, he lifted her from the bed and carried her into the shower. He held her as he washed her body in cool water since she was still warm from the release of her fire-gift.

"That cold water is heaven."

"Thought it might be. You're all pinked up again."

He soaped her gently between her legs and kissed her.

He must have felt her overall fatigue and weakness, because when her shower was done, he toweled her off then carried her back to bed where he tucked her in.

As she drifted off to sleep, she heard the showerheads crank up once more.

~ ~ ~

Late that afternoon, Jude woke up to an empty bed, but he caught the smell of bacon frying which sort of made up for it. Crisp bacon, one of his absolute favorite aromas. That, and coffee.

He also heard laughter and knew that Nathan was probably telling Hannah stories about him, no doubt revealing a drunken episode or two. He hoped his Executive Castle Coordinator was keeping it clean.

He slipped into a dark blue, silk robe only because he wasn't sure how Hannah would feel if she came back to the room and had to face all his nakedness first thing at night. Maybe she wouldn't have minded, but he didn't want to chance it.

He searched for and found his brush across the room by his dresser, no doubt having become dislodged the night before when he'd gotten rid of the comforter. He sat down on the end of the bed and began stripping his hair of tangles, usually a long process.

A knock on the door and Nathan entered with the Kellcasse Chronicle under one arm and looking worried, but bearing a cup of coffee.

As Jude took the mug, he asked, "What's going on?"

Nathan handed him the paper. "See for yourself. But I think we might need some big guns tonight to help us out of this one."

He set down his brush and laid the newspaper next to him so that he could see the entire front page. "Shit. Who took the picture?"

The shot was from Chelana and the groom was holding his bride, still unconscious. The photographer had zoomed in to show the two cuts on her neck with wound still seeping and the groom's white shirt covered in blood.

The headline didn't help. 'Near Massacre at Chelana while the Mastyr Plays in Love-nest with Human Bar-Maid.' Hannah must have hated reading that.

There was a picture of them kissing in the kitchen. Damn long-range photo lenses.

"Holy fuck."

"Yeah, that was my reaction."

He met Nathan's gaze. "Has Hannah seen this?"

"Of course. Her cheeks turned red, but her comment was to the point and ran something like 'This is so fucking unfair.'"

"She said 'fucking'?"

"Actually, she did. It was awesome."

"Okay, thanks. Tell her I'll be down in about half an hour. If anyone calls, just –"

"Oh, we've had calls today, mostly from the press and a couple leaving your basic *hate* messages. I suggested they call back later and that you were currently in meetings."

"Well done." He sipped his coffee, glancing at Nathan again. "You taking care of Hannah?"

"I prepared her a spinach omelet, and she said it was to die for. She didn't refuse one of Abigail's cupcakes either. Or the bacon. Not being light-sensitive, she's now out on the balcony, taking advantage of the last rays of the day."

He groaned inwardly. No doubt someone was taking pictures of her every move. "Stay with her and remind her that there will probably be photographers across the lake snapping away."

"I already told her, but she said she didn't care. She's pretty steamed. I like her."

When Nathan left, Jude scanned the article and it was what he'd come to expect from the Chronicle. There was a lot of shit about how Jude had let Kellcasse down *yet again* and how the mysterious mist at the wedding – also photographed – left a thousand unanswered questions. The newspaper had also made use of a really bad *double-entendre* in one of their photo captions. 'Was Mastyr Jude still *UP* to the job?' And of course, that was the exact phrase below the picture of the kiss. Bastards.

Jude was used to it, though. But right now he hoped Hannah had a thick skin because the fall-out had just begun and would get a lot worse before it got better.

Setting his mug on the dresser, he went back to de-tangling his hair. He pondered the difficulties of managing the mist situation as well as the volatile press that wouldn't hesitate to arouse public opinion against him so long as the articles sold more newspapers.

Even after he'd finished with his hair, he grabbed his coffee again and moved to sit on the end of the bed, holding his mug for a long time. He finally called the PR team leader, Frida, and had a brief discussion with her about tactics. They could easily head off the negative campaign, but Frida said the problem would be best handled with a show of increased Guard force, and that just adding the Shifter Brigade wouldn't be enough, especially since they were untried in the field. Could he bring in forces from another realm?

He gave it a lot of thought, and though he really didn't like the idea of having another mastyr around because of Hannah, he believed Frida was absolutely right. The papers would stir up a lot of hysteria, but troops on the ground would go a long way to easing the minds of most Kellcassians.

He called Malik, Mastyr of Ashleaf Realm, whose terrain, though denser with fewer canals and waterways, most resembled Jude's woodland and forest landscape.

"Malik, I need your help."

"Thought that might be why you called. The access point communication centers have already broadcasted the PR disaster in your realm. So what the hell is going on and what's with this mist, anyway?"

Jude gave him the rundown, adding that the wedding had been in the Chelana town square, a very public place, and photographers had taken pictures of much of the nightmare. When Margetta chose the public location, there had been no way to contain information about the current threat. "Mostly, I need a presence in Kellcasse, for the sake of helping my people to feel safe, and I'm asking if you'll come and bring part of your Ashleaf Vampire Guard with you."

"Of course I will. Ashleaf is very quiet at the moment, and it sounds like Margetta has her sights set on your realm."

"Great. Thank you. Go ahead and move your men into the bunkrooms at my training center. But hell, I'd really like a face-to-face, even for just a few minutes. If you could come to the castle grounds, say the peach orchard, then contact me telepathically, I could meet you there."

Malik chuckled. "I take it the rumors are true, that Hannah is a blood rose?"

Gossip traveled fast through the Nine Realms. "She is. There's no question about it." He put a hand to his stomach, stunned all over again that he had no pain anymore.

He told Malik about her essential fire-gift that Vojalie had said was very rare in the realm-world.

Malik whistled, then asked, "What's it like? The blood rose thing, I mean?"

The remaining mastyrs no longer asked whether their time would come, but *when*. Jude heard the anxiety in Malik's voice. None of the bonded mastyrs he knew had been prepared for the arrival of a blood rose, and each had faced a challenge in bringing a woman into his life.

So much had happened in the last two days that Jude had barely had time to process much of anything, and he really wasn't sure what to say to Malik. "It's extraordinary to have the blood-starvation resolved, I will say that. But I've never been so confused. I had my goals laid out, and you know my situation, but now everything is as unsettled as hell. But it's also true that you'll have a drive toward Hannah because I haven't bonded with her yet."

"Hence, a meet-up in the peach orchard."

"Exactly."

He'd confided in Malik more than once which was one reason he often called on him for help. He and Seth were his closest mates. Malik had known his wife and had been godfather to his daughter. He'd taken their deaths hard and like Jude had basically chosen to remain unattached while the Invictus and now their creator, Margetta, held sway.

"Just let me know when you've arrived and about when can you head over here?"

"Give me an hour. When I'm on my way, I'll contact Longeness and let him know."

"Sounds good."

He made his last call to the leader of the Kellcasse Civic Coalition, asking for a meeting with the twenty district leaders of his realm so that he could fill them in with accurate information. He also thought it would be a good thing to talk about Hannah and what she'd already done for the realm.

When he'd dressed in more formal realm-wear – black slacks and a dark blue silk shirt – he went in search of Hannah. Full-dark wouldn't arrive for some time in the northern realm. Because the steel shades were still down throughout his house, he contacted Hannah telepathically.

I'll be right in. Just catching the sunset.

As soon as she opened the balcony door and stepped across the threshold, his heart gave way. So much feeling surfaced that for a moment he couldn't move and he definitely couldn't speak.

But his expression must have caught Hannah off guard because as she closed the door, she asked. "What's wrong?"

He had to show her.

He crossed the room in a few brisk strides, hauled her into his arms and kissed her.

~ ~ ~

Hannah had never been more surprised than by this kiss. Jude had looked really upset for a good long moment when she'd opened the door from the balcony. Now she was in his arms, her heart beating hard in her chest. She'd wondered what it would be like to see him again after such extraordinary lovemaking earlier that morning.

Now she knew.

She slid her arms around his neck and responded in kind, stroking his back beneath his clasped Guardsman hair, nibbling at his lips, savoring when he drove his tongue against hers.

She hadn't expected to be caught up in an embrace first thing, but she loved it.

Her heart had warmed to Jude over the past two days. She'd longed for him before, and loved him very much as a good friend, but right now, oh, God, she was pretty sure she was falling in love with him, all the way, hard.

When he drew back, he looked as confused as ever as he pushed her hair away from her face. "I hadn't meant to do that, but the moment I saw you, it seemed like the only thing I could do."

"I've never had a more perfect greeting, and I mean that."

He kissed her again, and if Nathan hadn't been roaming the lower rooms, straightening up for the meetings, she felt certain they would have been headed for a quickie.

She almost suggested they retire once more to his bedroom, but Nathan came in and said that the Civic Coalition leaders had just started to arrive. "I'm making lots of coffee. You'd better go in and start laying feathers. You've got a couple trolls hop-stepping with steam coming out their ears. The same question keeps getting asked: 'Why weren't they told'?"

"Got it."

Despite Nathan's presence, Jude kissed her again, though this time, he didn't linger.

On her own, she returned to the balcony, enjoying the sun as it made its way slowly into the west. In early summer, this far north, it took a while for full dark to arrive. She pulled her phone from her jeans and called the Gold Rush. Amelia shut the door to her office against what sounded like a riotous, happy hour crowd so she could talk.

Hannah felt the smallest pang that she wasn't there. She knew so many people in Port Townsend and had as many human regulars as realm. More than one romance had blossomed, which reminded her that the bride who'd been assaulted by Margetta had announced her engagement at the Gold Rush.

"Sounds like the gang is all there."

"Yes, and that troll is back who gets stinking drunk then dances on the bar."

"You can't blame him. They use their feet for expression."

"It's a safety hazard," Amelia growled. Despite her overall free spiritedness, she had her rules and didn't like anyone overrunning them.

Hannah realized just how much she loved the kinds of problems she had at her bar compared to Jude's regular nightmare. Her heart felt crushed suddenly with the knowledge about how much her life had changed. She wanted to go back badly, to the way things were before the wraith-pair attacked Jude outside her bar.

Drawing her thoughts back to the Gold Rush, she said, "Well, have Hector keep an eye on him." Her bouncer could easily hold the troll in the air with one hand if he needed to. He was a Guardsman-sized shifter who'd fallen out with his pack and now lived in Port Townsend year round. Hannah had helped him get a special U.S. visa because he worked for her.

She trusted realm-folk, but like humans, sometimes alcohol could make them behave like idiots. And Hector, bless him, took care of business every night.

"He's already on it."

Hannah then explained what had been happening. Amelia whistled a couple of times then said she'd known a few things already because one of the fae had brought in a copy of the Kellcasse Chronicle. "Your ass looks stellar in that photo, by the way, and all your friends are going to be so jealous when they see that you're wrapped up in Mastyr Jude's arms."

A shiver went through her from pure desire that kept exploding in her chest for the vampire. Playing it safe, she said, "He's a good man and we're caught in something we're each trying to figure out. It's ... very realm." She hadn't gone into detail about her fire-gift. She couldn't quite bring the words to her lips.

Amelia was silent for a moment, then said, "Hannah, can I offer you a piece of advice?"

"Sure." Since her wild girlfriend and manager tended to speak way too much truth when she set her mind to it, Hannah wasn't all that anxious to hear her thoughts.

"Well, I've been wanting to say this to you for a long time, but here it is: You let that asshole, Mark Jackson, ruin you for other men. If it looks like Mastyr Jude, despite his exalted station as ruler of Kellcasse, wants to date you, then you should let him. You've kept yourself all bottled up. Mark was a control freak and Jude isn't. Despite the fact that he likes his way in most things, he always has an eye to what others need, and I know that would include you. And the Chronicle can just suck it."

Hannah had stopped breathing. All her old feelings of resentment and even fear about what Mark had done to her and his constant infringement on her freedom, made her tense up. At the same time, she knew Amelia was right. She'd let Mark's bad behavior affect her life and her choices way too much.

Could she have a life with Jude? But how would that work if she kept running her bar in Port Townsend while Jude fought the Invictus in Kellcasse? Of course, they did have one obvious thing in common: They both worked at night.

There was that.

"I'll think about what you've said, but I need you to know that I won't be back tonight, and I'm not sure when this situation will get resolved."

"I've got everything under control. We can talk each afternoon and if I need to pick up the slack on ordering, I can do that as well."

"I know you can. And thanks, Amelia. I knew I could rely on you."

When she hung up, she called Longeness and asked him to coordinate with Sandy, who supervised the communications center in her bar. Longeness, in true form, said he'd already made arrangements for Sandy to bring on another person to replace what Sandy called 'Hannah's hovering'.

Hannah laughed. "Okay, so I'm a little hands on."

Longeness laughed. "You're perfect. Don't ever change, and please ignore the Chronicle."

"I plan to. They're just trying to sell papers and incite tensions so they can sell even more papers."

"You got that right."

"And how's your wife?"

She heard a sigh that sounded very affectionate. "She's been having a lot of early labor. Her doctor thinks our boys will be here either this week or next."

The thought of babies, ready to be born, made her heart squeeze up really tight, and she had that horrible thought again, *How many babies did Jude want?*

When had she become so *female?*

"I hope you invite me to the baby-naming."

"We absolutely will. You know that."

She let her heart settle down then bid him good-bye.

The sun had finally dropped well below the horizon, and the stars were coming out. She left her sunning chair and moved back into the kitchen-living-area-combo, where Nathan was preparing a tray of dolma. She jerked her head in the direction of the living room. "How's it going in there?"

"Well, he got the trolls down from hop-stepping to just sliding their feet back and forth."

"That's a big improvement."

"He'll bring them round, especially with part of the Ashleaf Vampire Guard headed in soon. A bigger presence will help ease a lot of fears. Coffee?"

"Yes, thank you."

"I'll get you a fresh cup."

She had nothing to do now but wait until Jude finished up with his meeting. She moved to the window seat and sat down on the upholstered bench, one knee on the cushion, the other leg dangling over the side.

Nathan brought her the coffee, and she settled in to think and reflect, her gaze cast over the lake. There was no prettier view. Her improved realm vision saw more color than ever, even though it was nighttime. The lake appeared dark blue and the hills were made up of a variety of greens reflecting the shades of the various trees and shrubs. In addition, there were a lot of rhododendrons still flowering, which colored up the landscape with sprays of white, purple and pink.

But what charmed her the most were all the villages with lights glowing in windows and doorways, on streets, and patios. Not all realm-folk had excellent night-vision.

As she sipped, she felt her blood rose ability suddenly vibrate, a very soft sensation, but she couldn't quite understand the reason, unless of course Jude needed to feed. She hadn't really discussed with him how often he would need to tap into her vein. The very thought of his fangs biting her neck sent a surge of desire flowing through her, and once more her blood rose-ness responded. A flush drifted over her skin as well.

It would seem what she was as a blood rose also translated to her fire-gift.

Without giving it much thought, she set her coffee cup down and left the window seat. She headed out to the balcony, crossing to the far western side, which had a long flight of stairs broken by two landings.

But when she made her way down the stone steps, her heart suddenly felt laden again. Maybe Jude really did need to feed.

A walk might ease her. At least that's what her rational mind thought. But her body seemed to have a very dedicated purpose that had not yet translated to her brain.

She turned abruptly in a southwesterly direction. She'd never seen the place where Jude's wife and daughter were buried, though she knew it was in the orchard. But her thoughts weren't on Jude's grief-stricken past, but on something else she didn't understand. She felt really warm again, and the vein at her throat throbbed.

Then she realized that someone was already in the orchard.

Again, her feet seemed to know exactly where to go and before long she saw a Guardsman from behind, wearing the traditional coat, his long dark hair caught in a clasp at the back of his neck. Something about the set of his shoulders and his bowed head spoke to her of a kind of despair even Jude didn't possess. Her heart, always ready to jump with great tenderness to anyone in pain, started reaching toward him.

His shoulders straightened suddenly, and he looked around.

She aimed her telepathy at him. *I'm here.* Now, why had she spoken those words exactly?

When he turned in her direction, she recognized Mastyr Malik of Ashleaf Realm. Of course she knew him. He was one of

Jude's closest friends. He and Mastyr Seth of Walvashorr sat at the top of the list.

"Malik," she said, surprising herself that she'd addressed him so informally.

"Hannah? Sweet Goddess, stay back." He even held up a hand.

But her feet wouldn't let her do anything else but move in his direction. "I can feel your blood starvation. Let me take care of you?"

Her heart pounded now in her throat, and by the time she was teen feet away, she craved Malik, needed him, felt as though she'd die if he didn't come to her.

But he held out his palm and a soft blue light met her gaze, forcing her to stop, preventing her from reaching him no matter how hard she tried.

"Hannah, please stay were you are. Oh, Sweet Goddess, I can smell your blood." He looked as though he was in pain.

She had to breach the distance somehow, to give him what he needed. It was imperative for the entire realm that she serve him with her blood and her body.

If he wouldn't come to her, she wanted him to see her, so she stripped off her blouse.

"Hannah, don't!"

~ ~ ~

Jude held the door for the Civic leaders. He'd achieved what he'd wanted, their cooperation and understanding in a tough situation. And he'd been right about one thing; having Malik and part of his Guard already on the way had eased tensions like nothing else could have.

He'd also given them very specific descriptions of what the mist looked like and to have their county teams patrolling each village for any sign of mist and to alert the Kellcasse Communication Center no matter how insignificant the mist-sign might seem. He also knew there would be many false reports, but his Guardsmen flew fast and the shifter brigade could move like the wind, so he'd be able to put eyes on any sighting as soon as Margetta made another attempt.

But when he shut the door, Malik busted through his telepathy. *Get out to the orchard! I can't hold Hannah off much longer!*

Holy fuck! What was Hannah doing out there? He then realized he hadn't warned her. He'd been too caught up in kissing her that he'd forgotten to let her know Malik was coming and to stay away.

Jude ran to the side door, pulled it open, then flew as fast as he could into the orchard. A blue battle light guided him straight in, and he was shocked to find that Malik, sweating profusely with effort, was holding Hannah off with a low level of his battle frequency.

Taking hold of Hannah's arms from behind, he shouted, "Malik, get the hell out of here. Head to my training center. Fuck, I should have sent you there in the first place."

Malik didn't wait but launched into the air and disappeared.

He turned Hannah in his arms and saw the flush covering her bare neck and chest, and the vein pulsing at her throat. "Jude, help me. Please." She was breathing hard, struggling.

She wrapped her arms around his neck and kissed him. *Fuck me, Jude. Feed from me.* She was completely aroused and desperate, her breasts exposed, her nipples peaked. He groaned because he could smell her blood, that she'd created a fresh supply. He could also feel her agony because she'd been so caught up in her blood-rose-drive toward Malik.

I'll take care of you. He quickly unbuttoned and unzipped her jeans. He had to release her to get her shoes and pants off.

He caught her between her legs with his palm and she groaned as he massaged her. But his own need, with the smell of her blood in his nostrils, ramped up and he did his own unzipping.

Once he had his slacks below his ass, he backed her up to a tree but kept one arm behind her to cushion her. He lifted her hips with his free hand and she quickly wrapped her legs around his waist. When he guided his already stiff cock to her entrance and began to push inside, she groaned heavily.

He'd never been so out-of-control, so heated up in his life as he began to pump steadily.

Hannah was panting, her well gripping him and pulling on him, her need as profound as his own.

The smell of her blood, laced with the sweet scent of roses and the rich scent of the seashore, had him nuzzling her neck, licking up her vein.

"Jude, drink from me. My heart is full, ready for you."

He could feel that her supply had almost doubled and all because of Malik.

Some dark part of his brain filled with rage toward Malik that he'd been so close to Hannah, another mastyr ready to take his fill.

He pumped faster and deeper, needing Hannah to feel him and to know she belonged to him and to no other man. His mating frequency shot forward as well and penetrated her body, seeking her frequency. Finding it, he wrapped her up.

Take me, Jude. Help me. Take me. Her desperation fueled him.

He angled his head and struck her vein, hitting the right depth. He then formed a seal around the wounds with his mouth and began to suck. *You're mine, Hannah. You don't belong to anyone else. You're never to feed anyone else, share your body, or your mating frequency.*

She panted as she gripped his shirt, tearing at it, forcing the buttons to pop until she could push the fabric away and dig her nails into his shoulders. *I'm yours, Jude. I don't want anyone else. I'm yours, make me yours.*

He drank deeply for several minutes, holding his orgasm off. Waiting was damn hard, but he wanted to finish his feeding before he brought her to a climax.

She whimpered, as though in agony, but she panted throughout and didn't urge him.

When he'd had his fill and her heart had returned to normal, he drew back to look into passion-filled, violet eyes. He braced one arm on the tree above her head and as her legs gripped his waist, he began the push to the end.

He thrust with deep curls of his hips so that he could hit her just right. She held his gaze and he could sense her passion rising higher and higher until she was gasping for breath. "Jude, I'm ready."

He added a vibration to his cock, which made her gasp, then speeded up his thrusts. Her mouth opened and he quickly covered her lips with his hand. *You can scream against my palm.*

She let loose, and her body writhed against his as he pumped into her. Her orgasm put a fire deep in his sac, and the next moment, his release exploded through his cock, a lightning streak of pleasure so profound that he couldn't contain the roar. Hannah was his woman. He was marking her. She belonged only to him.

He kept roaring and Hannah screamed and cried out against his palm as ecstasy took him into the world beyond.

After a long moment, his body settled down and Hannah no longer panted.

But all was not well with her. He could feel it in his bones.

When he released her mating frequency, she uttered an unhappy, "Thank God for that."

He didn't know what exactly was wrong until she looked up at him with tears in her eyes. "Jude, I don't want this to be my life. I mean, I love having sex with you, but this is all too much. I was driven toward Malik the way I've been driven toward you. This isn't right, it isn't fair and it isn't what I want."

She pushed at his shoulders.

"Hold on for just a minute." He took off his torn shirt and as he eased out of her, he pressed his shirt between her legs. "I'm sorry, Hannah. I asked Malik to come to the orchard thinking you'd be well away from him. But I forgot to tell you he was coming. It didn't occur to me that you'd sense his presence and seek him out. This is my fault and I'm sorry."

Her shoulders drooped. "I think you missed my point. Jude, I absolutely hate not having control of my own life, my own destiny. And I want to go home. Now."

Chapter Seven

Hannah flew with Jude back in the direction of Port Townsend. He now wore his Guard uniform and frowned heavily. He wasn't a happy camper, but right now she didn't care.

After changing her clothes and packing up her things, she'd asked that he return her to the Gold Rush so that she could get back to her life. She was done with this horrible, sick situation. He'd just have to figure out some way of dealing with Margetta and her mist by himself. As for other mastyr vampires, Jude had better get his shit together and figure out how he and his men could keep her safe.

She was done.

She had her arm around his neck, but wished she didn't have to be so close to him.

The recent experience when she lost complete control of her will in facing Malik had thrown all her feel-good up into the air. She'd spoken exactly right when she'd said she hated not having control of her own destiny. But driven as she'd been toward Malik, made her distrust everything about her current experience with

Jude. How true were any of her emotions right now, or his? If they completed the blood-rose bond, would they suddenly discover they'd been tricked into a long-term relationship that neither of them really wanted?

If she understood the process, based on what the women on the loop said, once that bond was completed it would be permanent. And right now the only advantage she could see in having their mating vibrations lock into place, was ending forever her desire for other mastyr vampires or their drive toward her.

Big fucking deal.

She knew she wasn't entirely rational, but she was enraged by what had happened. She'd finally awakened to the reality that if she continued down this path, she'd bond with Jude just out of a desperate need to keep other mastyrs away from her.

All her options appeared to be gone.

Hannah, we can figure this out for you. I don't care about how this affects me, or having my blood-needs met. But I do care that you feel as though you've been stripped of your choices. What can I do to make this right?

Is that your phone ringing? she asked.

Yes, but I'm not going to answer it. He slowed his speed down. *Talk to me Hannah. Please. You're important to me on so many levels. You're my friend and I care about you. I know you didn't ask for this, but ...*

You're thinking about Margetta.

Hannah, we need you right now. At least until we get the mist thing figured out. I've put some of my best fae on the problem, and Vojalie said she would contact the Sidhe Council to see if a spell might be concocted to counter the mist's effects. This difficult situation is just temporary, but we need to stick together.

His words had a calming effect and she started to relax. She knew she was overreacting, but the events of the past two days had started taking a toll, and she didn't know just how much more she could take. She liked Mastyr Malik and knew him well because Jude had brought him to the Gold Rush at least a dozen times over the past couple of years. And she was completely embarrassed by her conduct and distressed that she'd caused Malik to feel an inappropriate drive toward her.

If he hadn't kept her away with a low setting of his battle frequency, she would have climbed all over him and begged him to feed.

And do other things.

Her cheeks grew hot and uncomfortable as she thought about it.

As Jude drew close to the access point, the guards waved them through. The tunnel of mist that made up the connecting point between worlds appeared and Jude flew them straight in.

But as they emerged from the mist tunnel, and Port Townsend came into view, Hannah gave a cry. A terrible black plume of smoke rose near the docks. "Jude, hurry. I have the worst feeling."

By the time they'd crossed half the distance over the Sound, Hannah felt her heart sink into her stomach. "The Gold Rush is on fire."

Once they were fifty yards away, Hannah asked Jude to remain in the air so she could see what was going on. She fished her phone from her pocket and realized she'd turned the ringer off and now had a dozen messages from Amelia and Sandy, no doubt telling her about the fire.

She couldn't believe what was happening. The blaze engulfed the entire building. Though two fire trucks sprayed massive amounts of water on the site, the building was too far gone for anything to be salvaged.

Her throat felt like she wore a noose.

But there was one thing she needed to know.

She called Amelia. The tough-as-nails woman who never cried could barely control her emotions as she spoke. “Hannah, I’m so sorry. I don’t know what happened. The smoke alarms went off then the automatic sprinklers. Everyone was racing to get outside not so much because of the fire, but because of the sprinklers. No one got hurt, thank God, but the fire spread so fast.”

“Did everyone get out?”

“I think so.” She took a moment to blow her nose. “All the staff, for sure. And I ran through the entire building, checking bathroom stalls, the supply closets, the bunkroom, everywhere that I could think of. By then, the fire just kept getting stronger even though the water was pouring all over everything. Hannah, even if the fire hadn’t destroyed most of your stuff, the water has done so much damage. I’m sick. I’m just so sick.

“The Fire Marshall is pretty sure it was arson. By his guess, someone poured accelerant all around the outside of the building. He can’t account for a sudden, engulfing blaze otherwise. But there will be an investigation. He even asked if you had enemies.”

Did she have enemies? Just one major piece-of-work that moved with a beautiful golden light and created mist from her limbs. It didn’t take a genius to figure out who was behind this blatant attack on her. But what did Margetta hope to gain by burning down the Gold Rush? It was just a bar. A human bar.

And it was really important to Hannah.

Maybe that was the point. Margetta had hit her where it hurt.

"Where are you?" Hannah asked, searching the crowd below. Needless to say, people had come from all over to witness what for most would probably be a once in a lifetime event. "I'm in the air with Mastyr Jude. Wave if you can."

"Okay, I'm waving."

The police cars at the scene had taped off a long section around the building to keep the people back, so it took a few seconds to finally see Amelia flipping her arm back and forth. Somehow it eased her to see her manager waving. "I see you. I'll join you in a minute."

Still holding Jude's neck, she shoved her phone back into her pocket.

~ ~ ~

Jude felt something important slipping away from him so fast that his brain scrambled. It had been such a long time since he'd been this close to a woman that he'd honestly forgotten how to function, how to think in terms of her, how to react.

Despite the fact that in his gut he knew he was doing the wrong thing, he did it anyway and pulled Hannah close. "I can't let you go. You have to stay with me. At least for now."

She pulled her arm from around his neck. "I need to be with my people. Their lives have been turned upside down. My entire staff. And by the way, Amelia said there was no reason for the fire and that the captain said it was probably arson. Of course we both know who's behind this. But what I don't get is why Margetta gives a rat's ass about the Gold Rush, unless she's just a vindictive bitch besides being a flaming psychopath. And if I hadn't had the sprinklers in order, everyone inside would have died. You have to let me go."

Her eyes were wild and she started pushing against him. She had no real physical ability to escape his hold, but she pushed anyway. "Hannah, don't do this."

"Let me go, Jude, please. Cut me some slack. I just lost my bar."

"We'll replace it, Hannah, I promise you. We know who's at fault here, which is one more reason to stick together right now. Margetta is a psycho but she's also deliberate in what she does. She had a reason for doing this."

"Put me down now!"

Jude felt desperate. He didn't know how to reach Hannah, though he sure as hell didn't blame her for fighting.

He saw something flash at the corner of his eye. Turning to look, he saw nothing, but he almost lost hold of Hannah, who started slipping down his body. He caught her quickly.

She yelled at him. "What are you doing? You know I can't fly. You have to lower me to the parking lot."

"I thought I saw something."

"You did: My life burned to the ground."

When he heard the catch in her voice, he realized that tears were rolling down her cheeks.

But another flash distracted him. Yet, once more when he turned to look, nothing was there. What the hell was going on?

"Why are you shifting around in that weird way?"

"Because something realm is here and it's not good."

"Just let me go."

He heard the sadness and the resignation in her voice. He hated that his life had intruded on hers in such a way that she'd lost so much.

"Fine, but let me come with you."

He descended slowly, dropping down between a row of cars. But as soon as he released her, she sprinted away. He followed swiftly after, but just like that three wraith-pairs appeared in front of him, cutting him off.

"Hannah!" he shouted, knowing full-well that the burning of the Gold Rush was just a ploy and that she was in danger. But she didn't respond.

The Invictus began releasing red streaks of battle energy, so that he had no way to get to Hannah except through them. He raised his blue energy shield, which when struck by the wraith-pairs' energy, deflected and started bouncing off cars, making a fireworks show out of the parking lot.

He switched to battle mode and focused only on the work that needed to be done in front of him. If he worked fast, maybe he could reach Hannah before anything happened to her.

He geared up and sent energy bursts in quick succession that struck the wraiths and their mates. Two pair fell prone immediately.

He wasn't a mastyr for nothing.

But the remaining Invictus pair fought on, more cunning than the two that had fallen. Then suddenly a golden light appeared and in a flash that almost blinded him, all three pair were swept across the Sound toward the access point.

In that moment, he knew he was too late.

"Hannah!" he shouted.

He rose into the air, searching for her, but didn't see her anywhere. "Hannah!"

The gold light returned. "She can't hear you, Jude. She's already halfway across Kellcasse by now. I found a lesser Mastyr looking for a nice hook-up, who happily tagged along and took Hannah into your realm. He'll be pleased about the boost in power when he bonds with your woman. It's just too bad you couldn't control her."

And just like that, the gold light winked out and Margetta was gone.

A strong ocean breeze off the Strait blew across Jude's back. He rose high in the air once more, higher and higher, and away from the crowds that had gathered to watch him battle the Invictus.

Now he was just alone, levitating above the last flickers of the burning bar and the sound of the water still being sprayed over the collapsed building.

He made his way back across the Sound in the direction of the access point. When he arrived, he found the access point guards dead, their throats cut, and showing no signs of having fought back.

Margetta had brought her mist and killed again.

He reached for Malik telepathically, and a moment later, Malik opened his mind. *Jude. Everything okay?*

We've got a disaster. He then gave him a brief update. *I have to find Hannah.*

I'll let Longeness know what's going on.

Good place to start, but I've got to think.

Jude slowed his flight as he shut the communication with Longeness down, knowing he was in a state of shock. That old expression rose within his mind that he'd just had the rug pulled out from under him.

He needed to find his footing and he needed it fast. He pathed Malik this time. *Meet me on the balcony at Castle Island.*

I'm two minutes out.

Taking the first step helped to center his brain. He wasn't sure what he was going to do yet, but talking things over with a fellow mastyr often brought clarity.

He picked up his speed and flew faster than he ever had before, rising high into the air to avoid trees or hills or any of his Guardsmen out on patrol.

A few minutes later, he touched down on the stone pavers of his castle house.

Malik was there, his expression intent, eyes wild. "I can't believe this happened."

Jude shook his head. "I know. I'd expected another mist attack, but not Margetta, arson, and the Gold Rush."

Malik frowned. "It's not like you to let something like this take you by surprise. What happened?"

Jude shoved his hand through his hair, dislodging the woven clasp. "Hannah was really distressed, demanding to be taken home after what happened here." He waved in the direction of the peach orchard. "She didn't even want me around. I couldn't make sense of what I needed to say to her. It all turned into a fight, and I was completely distracted when Margetta, through these brief flashes of light, brought in three wraith-pairs." He gritted his teeth. One of the worst things a Guardsman could ever do was get distracted.

Now Hannah was in the clutches of a madwoman.

Jude leaned over the railing, the woven clasp in his hands. "And the fuck if I know what to do."

Malik put his hand on Jude's shoulder. "Your men and mine are out hunting for her now. If she's anywhere in the realm, we'll find her. Be patient."

Patient. Sweet Goddess, his heart was banging around in his chest so hard that his ribs hurt. He couldn't bear the thought of Hannah suffering because of Margetta's insanity.

He took several deep breaths, forcing his heart to calm down so that he could think straight. Hannah was a survivor and quick on her feet. She would find a way to stay alive if she could. And she had power, more than she knew. He had to trust in that, and trust in her ability to manage herself until he could find her.

At the very least, he could try to contact her telepathically, though he had no way of knowing if Margetta could intercept their mind-to-mind conversation. He decided to take the leap anyway. Best case scenario, Hannah might be able to tell him where she was.

Hannah, he sent through the airwaves. *Hannah? Can you hear me?*

Jude, thank God. I don't know what to do.

Jude recalled that a mastyr had taken her. *Has that vampire hurt you?*

What?

The mastyr that abducted you. Did you have a drive toward him like you did with Malik?

Yes, but then I thought of you and it gave me the strength to bring forward my fire-power. I scorched him so he's leaving me alone for now.

Jude couldn't help it. He smiled. *Proud of you.*

Jude, you need to stay away from me. Margetta's here and she's waiting for you. It's a trap. A big one. She doesn't know it, but I can see that she has a hundred wraith-pairs hidden behind some kind of cloak. Please don't come after me. It's you she wants dead.

Jude stood upright and began pulling his hair back, securing the clasp once more. He turned to meet Malik's intense, brown eyes, then relayed what Hannah had just told him.

"Can you find out where she is?" Malik asked.

"I will. But none of our guardsmen or the shifters will be able to find them. Margetta has a powerful shield in place."

"Sweet Goddess."

"Just give me a moment." Jude recalled what it had been like to find his wife and daughter murdered in the peach orchard. In that split-second, his life had altered completely.

The same thing was happening to him right now, that all the events of the past two days had overturned his desires and life completely. He just hadn't seen it.

His mind finally pulled together as he realized that the passion that had erupted so swiftly between Hannah and himself wasn't because she was a blood rose. He'd been in love with her for months, possibly even years.

During all that time, she'd filled a hole in his life long before he'd taken her into his bed. She'd been his friend and his coworker, and a couple times when he'd been drunk, she'd put him to bed in the bunkroom. He'd told her then that he loved her. He remembered that much, despite his beer-blasted mind, but he'd pretended later that the words hadn't been said.

His heart began to warm with long-suppressed feelings. He'd held to his commitment not to become involved with another woman until the Invictus were ground into the earth. How ironic that in this case, if he'd obeyed his heart and bonded with Hannah, she wouldn't be in Margetta's clutches. Their unity would have protected them both. He wouldn't have been distracted and they could have faced the fire at the Gold Rush together.

Instead, her fear of being controlled and his resistance to loving her had brought just enough of a divide that Margetta had been able to walk right in and abduct her.

His chest grew tight. His eyes burned. What would he do if anything happened to her? He didn't think he could bear losing a second wife.

As soon as that exact phrase went through his mind, he knew he'd been fooling himself about Hannah because he already thought of her as his woman and, yes, his wife. And he'd felt that way for a long time.

And of course it was just like her, the selfless person he knew her to be, to tell him not to come to her aid and that he'd be walking into a trap. Hannah had one of the most generous spirits he'd ever known. She was a woman of fire and of great power because of that spirit. Her current gift merely reflected who she was in her life.

He met Malik's gaze once more. "I'm going to find out where she is, and if I have to, I'll take her place in Margetta's little drama."

Malik stared at him for a long, hard moment, then straightened his shoulders as though preparing for battle. *Do what you need to do. I've got your back.*

Jude loved the brotherhood of his fellow mastyrs.

Nodding once, Jude turned inward. *Hannah, I'm coming for you if I have to hunt through this realm day-and-night. And you don't get a say in that. But I'd rather find you right now when I'm powered by the blood you shared with me, than struggle for hours to get your location. I have Malik with me and we'll bring all our forces to bear on Margetta's army. Remember, I've been battling Margetta and her kind of two hundred years, so please tell me where you are.*

~ ~ ~

Hannah stood at the foot of the beautiful stone bridge Jude had shown her the night before when he'd flown her through his realm. Should she just tell him where she was?

The mastyr who had abducted her from Port Townsend, lay burned and shivering at her feet. The moment he'd touched down ready to drink from her, she'd made her decision and let loose with a swathe of flames that fried him. She couldn't have done it sooner or she would have fallen to her death.

Margetta, who stood ten feet away, had merely laughed, uninterested in the suffering Hannah had just caused one of her minions.

However, when she'd tried to use her fire-power on Margetta, she'd failed.

At first she didn't understand why, but after a few minutes, she could feel a powerful stream of energy aimed at Hannah, one that kept Margetta safe. The ancient fae had found a way to protect herself.

She knew she was bait in a trap meant for Jude. She also understood that his death would be a powerful coup for Margetta, a way to incite fear within the citizens of Kellcasse and make it easier for her to take over the realm.

But Hannah debated, not wanting Jude to be hurt or killed. She knew him, though, and that what he'd said was true. He would never stop hunting for her. So how much better if he arrived at the height of his strength instead of worn down by hours of searching his realm for her?

Hannah also knew that she and Jude had power together, but did they have enough to escape a battleground like this one with at least a hundred wraith-pairs in the air and on the ground, all hidden by Margetta?

Glancing at the ancient fae, Hannah saw the killing mist drifting from Margetta's lower limbs, ready to release as needed.

And in that moment, she made her decision, and contacted Jude. *All right. I'm on board. But you need to know that Margetta's ready to mist the whole area. I can see it forming on her. And Jude, I can't use my fire-gift against her. She's blocking me somehow.*

I understand. But I still insist on coming. And I'm not alone. Again, Malik is here and that is something Margetta may not know, that another mastyr is in the realm to help direct both the Vampire Guard and the Shifter Brigade. We're working together and I believe we can do this. Can you trust me?

Hannah didn't want to die. That's what she knew. She also didn't want her time with Jude to end. Another absolute truth.

When she'd found herself whisked away in the air by a vampire with almost as much speed as Jude, she'd sunk to the bottom of the hole she'd fallen into. She had extraordinary gifts that she wanted no part of, an erotic relationship with Jude that threatened her way of life in Port Townsend, and a bar that had just burned to the ground.

And now she stood at the point of death with Margetta holding a metaphorical sword to her neck.

Yet, in all of this what she wanted the most was for Jude to survive at all costs. He was what mattered. Not her bar, or her fear of her emerging gifts, or her anxiety that she might lose control of her life.

In that moment, she'd finally risen above all her fears.

Taking a deep breath, and praying she was making the right decision, she pathed, *Do you remember that place that you pointed out last night, the beautiful wide canal with the stone bridge and unique finials along both railings? The bridge that joins two different communities?*

Yes, of course. Kelltah Bridge.

That's it. I just couldn't think of the name. Well, I'm standing at the foot of the bridge on the eastern side. Margetta is maybe ten or so feet away from me.

I'm on my way.

Hannah couldn't help the tears that tracked down her cheeks. She trembled now, not for herself but for Jude. She gazed in an arc skyward over all the wraiths and their mates waiting for Margetta's command. But how were Jude and his forces supposed to combat an invisible enemy especially if Margetta released her mist?

Margetta called to her. "You should reach out to Jude and bring him here. He would come if you said the word."

Apparently, the bitch couldn't read all telepathic conversations, or maybe she just had to be tuned in.

Margetta smiled. "By the way, I enjoyed your little show in the peach orchard. Made me hungry for my dear Gustav. I almost called off the whole operation but chose to ignore my lusts. If you'd had enough self-control, Hannah, you wouldn't be here right now. Stupid mistake leaving Jude's side. But I figured, you, being human, would falter sooner than later."

Hannah kept her gaze fixed anywhere but on the ancient fae. She remained stoic, although it didn't help her nerves that she stood over a burned up, but-healing-swiftly mastyr vampire, who occasionally growled up at her. At least once she'd fried him, her blood rose drive toward his mastyr status had dropped to almost nothing.

Jude would arrive soon, but then what?

She dreaded the moment, yet couldn't wait to see him again.

Word must have spread that the mist had arrived in the two villages. The whole area felt like a ghost town and Hannah suspected the occupants had slipped away into the surrounding woodlands, hidden in caves, or anywhere else they could hide.

At least the populous was relatively safe.

But it was an eerie scene with just Margetta, the toasted vampire still lying prone and moaning occasionally, and of course the hidden army. Very eerie.

Jude arrived flying in from the south. As he drew close he looked as magnificent as ever, his Guardsman coat flapping behind him, the silver medallions down each side of his thigh boots winking from the lamppost light all along the bridge.

"Ah, and here comes your lover."

Margetta had said it exactly right.

Her lover. The man she loved. The one she belonged to.

Jude had tried to warn her to stick close when he held her in the air above the burning wreckage of her bar. But the sight of what she loved sinking to a massive pile of wet, unpleasant ashes had messed with her head, maybe just as Margetta knew it would.

She'd essentially lost her mind.

Now she was here.

While hovering in the air a few feet above the ground, Jude approached Margetta. When he was almost within touching distance, he said, "I'll take her place. Just let her go. I know it's me you want."

But Margetta laughed at him, snapped her fingers, and several wraith-pairs descended on him, binding him with ropes. They dragged him onto the bridge and tied him to a lamppost.

Jude, what are we going to do?

Hannah, there's something I need you to know.

She was too far away from him. She whipped toward Margetta. "Please let me say good-bye. Please."

"How touching, and I'll grant you this wish, because you're going to die with your mastyr tonight."

Another snap of her fingers and wraith-pairs flew low and grabbed Hannah beneath her arms. She felt the charred vampire reach for her foot but miss as she became airborne.

The next moment, she was next to Jude. She took his face in her hands and pressed herself up against him. *I love you and I'm sorry. This is my fault.*

He drew back slightly. *Hey, no one's to blame. This is war, and we can't always predict what happens next. You've done beautifully in a horrendous situation. I'm so proud of you.*

She nodded, but tears ran down her cheeks. She would have kissed him again, but the wraith-pair bound her as well, securing them together.

I love you, Hannah. I've loved you for years. I've just been lying to myself. All those times I came into your bar just to accompany my men for some R & R, but in reality I couldn't wait for the moment I'd spend even a handful of minutes chatting with you. I watched you all the time.

You know I felt the same way.

Hannah, I'm so sorry for all of this. If I'd understood that my growing affection and desire for you would incite your blood-rose and fire-gifts, I would have stayed away from Port Townsend. I didn't want this for you, and the Goddess knows the sight of your bar burning to the ground has made me question everything I've done, every decision I've made.

Hannah listened and her throat grew even tighter. Margetta had transformed into the wraith that she was, being both fae and wraith. She flew back-and-forth over the bridge in her red gauzy dress and began ranting at Jude, expounding on her great plans for the Nine Realms, how one day all would bow before her magnificence.

Hannah ignored her. Instead, she forced herself to face the truth about her feelings for Jude.

She loved him.

She loved him with all her heart.

And now her own willfulness had landed him here, bound to her, and soon to be executed.

With Margetta clearly enjoying the sound of her own voice, and appealing to her army of wraith-pairs at the same time, Hannah pathed, *I love you, too, Jude. I think it's been forever for me as well, much longer than just the past few months that followed the awakening in the supply closet.*

He held her gaze. *You could have been scrubbing the floor behind the bar when that happened, and I would still consider it one of the best moments of my life.*

Jude. Her telepathic voice was little more than a whisper. *I've been a fool through this process. I kept holding onto my freedom because of a difficult past experience. But you always kept my freedom at the top of your list. Now, I have no freedom at all.*

She felt him reaching toward her with his hand and she struggled in the bindings to meet him halfway. When her fingers touched his, it was magic all over again.

A vibration she could only call 'love' swept through her, cleansing her of past suffering and freeing her to open her heart fully to Jude.

Mist began drifting stronger out of Margetta as she flew.

It wouldn't be long now. Jude would soon be unconscious and Margetta would kill them both.

Jude's voice pierced her head. *Hannah, bond with me. No matter what happens, I don't want anything else but to feel close to you right now.*

She leaned her head against his. All her doubts were gone. *I want to more than anything in the world.*

~ ~ ~

As Margetta waxed on about her magnificence, Jude was right there with no hesitation. He sent his mating frequency barreling through her chest and pushing inside hers. She moaned, her head falling back. *Jude, that feels extraordinary.*

He found her own mating vibration pulsing in soft receptive waves. He surrounded her deep inside her body-and-spirit combined, wrapping her up in his love and letting her feel with every ounce of strength how much he loved her.

Why did I hesitate? he said. *This is incredibly beautiful.*

As the frequencies began to pulse in rhythm together, Jude gave himself completely and felt Hannah do the same in return.

The bond suddenly locked in place. Hannah cried out, though Jude noted her shout didn't stop Margetta. Instead, the army Hannah had seen now became perfectly clear to Jude. He felt Hannah's power become his, which was something he hadn't expected.

Hannah, your fire-gift is in me now, and I can see through Margetta's shield. I can see her army.

I can feel it as well and that we're one. It's amazing. And I can feel what you're feeling, and how the ropes are digging into your wrists. But, Jude, what are you thinking?

That I might be able to withstand Margetta's mist and make use of your fire-gift. I can feel the heat down both my arms and my palms are tingling.

I know that feeling well.

He added, *I can also feel that she is blocking your gift but she has no such protection against me.*

So we have a shot.

I think we do, but let me contact Malik first, and give him a heads-up.

I'll wait for your orders.

Jude almost smiled, but he didn't want to alert the witch still flying back and forth, who was all worked up into a frenzy as she went on and on about her plans for ruling the Nine Realms.

Malik? Jude pathed.

I'm right here. I have both villages surrounded, but at a considerable distance. Are you sure Margetta's army is in place?

Jude lifted his gaze, scanning the night sky and the army now visible to him. He strove to send the images to Malik, which was something he wasn't sure he could do. But he tried anyway. *Does any of that come through?*

Hell, yeah, it does! But, how are you doing this?

It's because of Hannah. We've bonded, and in about thirty seconds we're going to break out of these ropes, and I'm going to attack the ancient fae. She'll probably release the rest of her mist, but I can feel within myself that I'm sharing Hannah's abilities and one of them is her very human resistance to the killing mist. At the same time, both her forces and ours won't be immune, so it will be an even playing field. Just be ready.

Got it.

Alert the troops, and when you see me go after Margetta, she should lose power and the shield should drop and her army become visible, then it's all up to you. Take out as many wraith-pairs as you can.

With fucking pleasure.

He returned his attention to Hannah. *You ready to break out?*

Absolutely.

Then let's do it.

He accessed the fire-gift and felt sudden heat jump from his skin and start to work on the ropes. Ten seconds later, he was free. Without waiting, he launched at Margetta, catching her in the air and dragging her into the canal below.

She became a wild, fighting thing, but he held onto her as long as he could, releasing the fire even below the surface, at the places where he held her.

She screamed, then dragged in a lung-full of water.

The next moment, she simply disappeared. Gone.

Jude surfaced fast, rising into the air as he breached the canal, heading back to Hannah. She had flames shooting from her palms, spreading them in an arc to hold back five wraith-pairs determined to get to her.

Jude came at them from behind, adding his own fire and scorched them, one after the other, until they were screaming and throwing themselves into the canal.

He took his place next to Hannah, holding her close, because right now his Guardsman and Shifter Brigade as well as Malik's forces converged and began battling wraith-pairs.

The night sky had never been full of so many blue and red flashes.

"Jude, look, off to the northeast."

He glanced in the direction of her raised arm and watched as one by one wraith-pairs started vanishing mid-fight.

"She's saving as many as she can. Should we go after her?"

He shook his head. "The level of her power is still unknown, which means I have no intention of putting you in harm's way. Right now, you're my priority."

~ ~ ~

Hannah's heart beat so hard in her chest that she had a difficult time catching her breath. She'd gone from just enjoying her day-to-day, and all her friends and customers who came to her bar, to watching two armies battling on the ground and in the sky.

More than one wraith-pair tried to reach Jude, but shifters and vampires alike headed them off.

A lot of death followed, but that couldn't be helped.

This was war.

And to the degree that she was a blood rose and now bonded to a powerful Mastyr Vampire, this was her war as well. Yet somehow it fit, as though all her experience at the Gold Rush, growing up there and having a father who embraced the Nine Realms, had prepared her for exactly this day, or rather *night*.

She no longer saw the worlds as separate, but moving fluidly back and forth, something that would increase as the decades moved along. They were different species yet shared enough DNA to build lives together and to create families.

As the last of the distant wraith-pairs vanished because of Margetta's continued, though hidden presence, and one of Malik's

Guardsmen defeated the sole remaining wraith-pair on the bridge, Hannah could finally breathe.

Jude had already called in for medical teams. The policy in the Nine Realms had changed since Samantha had become bonded to Mastyr Ethan of Bergisson Realm. She had the power to dissolve the hated bond between wraith and realm-mate. Any surviving wraith-pairs would be turned over to Ethan for long-term rehabilitation.

When Malik dropped down to join them, Hannah tensed up immediately, concerned that she would have the same overpowering desire toward him that she'd experienced before.

But nothing happened. Only a sudden vibration deep within that spoke of the bond she shared with Jude, now inviolable, permanent, and powerful.

And the question she'd been asking for months, as in how many babies Jude wanted, didn't seem so absurd anymore. It made sense, and a new kind of desire rose within her filled with purpose and love. She wanted to have a family with Jude. That's how far around the globe she'd traveled in two brief nights.

Jude, maybe sensing the direction of her thoughts, hugged her tighter about the waist. *I'm feeling something beautiful from you right now, and it's making me want to take you to bed.*

She leaned up and kissed him, then stared into dark gray eyes. *And that's exactly where I want to be with you.*

He turned to Malik. "I want to get Hannah home. Will you see to our troops?"

Malik clasped Jude on the shoulder. Hannah thought he looked incredibly sad as he smiled. "Of course I will."

She watched as for a long moment, the two realm leaders stayed in that position, staring at each other until Jude nodded slowly. She wasn't sure if Jude had communicated telepathically with Malik or not, but she doubted the moment needed words. They were brothers-in-arms, who'd been fighting the same battle for a very long time.

Malik turned to her. "Good-night, Hannah. I'll be seeing you soon, I'm sure."

"Of course. You're always welcome at the Gold Rush." Reality descended abruptly, but what had been so devastating a few hours ago, now seemed softened by her commitment to Jude. "Although, you might want to wait until it's rebuilt."

"Which it will be right away," Jude added, meeting Hannah's gaze. "I'll get my best troll and elven contractors on it."

Hannah often used realm workers and contractors for her bar and her home. They did a wonderful job every time.

When Jude moved his hand from around her waist, she understood the signal and positioned herself on his booted foot. She slid her arm around his neck, and he pulled her tight against his side. After bidding Malik farewell, Jude took off, lifting her into the air.

And Hannah smiled.

~ ~ ~

Jude could feel the shift in Hannah as though it was written in every breath she breathed. The bond allowed him to feel what she was feeling, and for the last few minutes on the bridge, he'd felt her mating vibration begin to hum on a different frequency than before. And it felt full of life and intent.

As he flew toward Castle Island, he felt as though he held all of life in his arms, something rich and bountiful, a kind of necessary excess meant to feed the soul.

He drew in deep breaths. He was *all men* in this moment, both real and a representation of what it meant to be male, to have a woman in his arms, and to feel her need to give the universe rebirth.

When he arrived, Nathan greeted them both with anxious grips of hands and thanksgiving that Margetta had seen a defeat at Kelltah Bridge.

"How do you already know?"

"It's all over Realm-You-Tube. Some troll kid, who will probably be flayed by his parents later, used his cellphone to film the battle. But it's a good thing, trust me. I've been on the phone for the past forty-five minutes with Council Leaders. There are celebrations all over the Realm tonight, and tomorrow you and Hannah will both be hailed as heroes. So where are you going to celebrate?"

Jude just looked at him, and since he still had his arm tight around her waist, Nathan nodded. Then he grinned. "I have a surprise waiting for you in the bedroom. In the meantime, I hear that all the bars in Kelltah will be open the rest of the night and even into the day for some of us sunlight-friendly realm-folk." He shrugged into a black leather jacket and smoothed the sides of his hair back. "My ride's here."

He winked and turned in the direction of the front door.

"Elena?" Jude asked.

"Yep. Abigail gave her a few days off."

"I guess we won't be seeing much of you."

Nathan, halfway to the front door, called back, "And something tells me that's the way you'd want it right now. Plenty of provisions in the fridge. See ya in three days."

Jude laughed.

"So what do you think Nathan left for us, in the bedroom, I mean?" Hannah asked.

"I don't know, but I'm sure it will taste incredible."

Turned out, he left a platter of fruit, whipped cream, and champagne. Maybe a little cliché, but it worked.

Hannah insisted on removing his boots, touching each silver medallion as she did so. He wasn't sure why she liked them, so he asked.

She sighed. "Don't ask me why, but they're sexy as hell. Or maybe it's the leather, or maybe you. Actually, I think it's the whole package."

A kiss almost led to rolling around on the floor then and there, but Jude wanted more. This would be their first time as a bonded couple, and he wanted to do it right.

Besides – and this was no small thing – he needed a shower.

He left Hannah to enjoy his numerous shower heads while he traipsed off to one of the guest room showers. He felt almost dizzy as he entered the first bedroom, which was the one that had been Joy's room. And something that felt very fae came over him. He saw three children on the floor, two boys with dark, curly hair and the third a girl with straight brown hair and violet eyes. They were playing a U.S. board game called Monopoly.

They all turned and looked at him.

"Hi, Dad," the girl called out.

He drifted sideways and fell against the doorjamb.

The vision lasted only a few seconds more, but in that time, the world flipped on its axis and tears started to well in his eyes. He blinked hard, then closed them firmly because he was still dizzy.

But when he opened his eyes, another vision came of Naomi and Joy, standing where the children had been playing. *We wish you well, Jude. Our loving best while you finish your years with Hannah and your new family. They both blew kisses, which was something they'd always done when he'd head out to work for the night.*

When the second vision ended, he begged the Goddess, "No more. My heart will fail."

He heard feet running down the corridor and turned to find Hannah racing toward him, wrapped up in a towel.

"Jude, what is it? I felt such grief and joy pouring from you. What happened? What's the matter?"

And this was why he loved her as much as he did. She was with him, had always been with him, and always would be.

He caught her up in his arms and held her fast. "I love you, Hannah. You have my heart. You are my heart."

She drew back and met his gaze, nodding her understanding several times. After a moment, she pulled out of his arms and took his hand. "Come join me in your shower. I don't know what just happened, but you need to be with me right now. We need to be together."

Because he could still feel the past and future still lingering in the bedroom that had once belonged to his daughter, he agreed and walked her back to his bedroom.

Later, after showering with Hannah, Jude stood at the foot of the bed and worked carefully at popping the champagne cork. Hannah arranged the comforter to create a makeshift table on the bed for the platter of fruit and whip cream.

The loud pop, made Hannah laugh.

With his heart full, he poured out two glasses, then drew close. Handing her one, he said, "To a bond I'll always treasure."

And she replied, "To a bond that has already blessed me more than I can say."

She fed him fruit covered in whipped cream, and he returned the favor, sharing kisses in between, touches, gentle fondling, and a slow build.

With the fruit consumed and the glasses empty, Jude set the platter aside and tossed the comforter on the floor. He stretched out beside Hannah and kissed her, a long, lingering kiss that became more as he pressed his tongue against her lips. She parted for him, sighing as he slid his tongue inside her waiting mouth.

His mating vibration, now attached to hers in the mysterious realm way, hummed and stroked her at the same time. She cooed her pleasure. *That feels so good within me, Jude. I had no idea it would be like this. And I can feel what you're feeling.*

Same here. I love you, Hannah.

I love you, too.

He moved onto her and she spread her legs for him so that what was already hard found her entrance and pushed inside. Her hips rocked as he glided along her wet pathway, feeling her well tug on him, while he moved his tongue slowly in and out of her mouth.

~ ~ ~

Hannah loved the weight of Jude on top of her, the muscular frame that she'd been lusting after for so long. He was inside her now, driving steadily, working her deep. She'd longed for this connection without understanding the why of it.

And now that she'd endured the difficulties of the past two nights with him, she felt deeply changed in a way that had shifted her life forever.

She wrapped both arms around his neck and held him tight, wanting him to feel with every undulation of her body that she loved him, that she always would.

The bonding on Kelltah Bridge had begun a process that making love with him now completed.

With her hands, she stroked his shoulders then the full length of his powerful arms. She savored his strength, valuing that what had been given to him was used nightly to save his people.

She drew back and met his gray eyes. "You've changed everything in the best way possible. You are my fire."

He moaned and kissed her hard, his hips curling deeper into her, moving faster. She swept with him to the point of ecstasy, and with the blood rose bond and the vibrations that they both released, before long she was crying out. At the same time, Jude roared, that guttural animal sound that swept through her body, telling her that she belonged to him, only to him.

Much later, after he'd made love to her repeatedly, pleasuring her body in every possible way, and after he'd fed from her a second time, he fell asleep in her arms.

But for Hannah, sleep didn't come right away. Instead, she gently rubbed the back of his neck beneath the mass of his hair, as tears streamed down the sides of her face into her pillow. She had lost the Gold Rush, if only for the moment, but gained a treasure of infinite value.

She knew Jude would rebuild her bar, but this time she intended to turn more of the responsibility over to her manager, who'd been begging for the last couple of years to play a bigger role anyway.

Time to let go.

Time to embrace the future.

"You're my fire, Jude," she whispered against the soft sounds of his breathing. "You're my fire."

Thank you for reading **EMBRACE THE NIGHT**! In our new digital age, authors rely on readers more than ever to share the word. Here are some things you can do to help!

Sign up for my newsletter! You'll always have the latest releases, hottest pics, and coolest contests!

http://www.carisroane.com/contact-2/

Leave a review! You've probably heard this a lot lately and wondered what the fuss is about. But reviews help your favorite authors -- A LOT -- to become visible to the digital reader. So, anytime you feel moved by a story, leave a short review at your favorite online retailer. And you don't have to be a blogger to do this, just a reader who loves books!

Enter my latest contest! I run contests all the time and have been known to mail out a dozen packages in a month. Check out my contest page today!

http://www.carisroane.com/contests/

Also Available: Book #6, Malik and Willow's story: EMBRACE THE WILD!!!

Also, be sure to check out the Blood Rose Tales – TRAPPED, HUNGER, and SEDUCED -- shorter works set in the world of the Blood Rose, for a quick, satisfying read.

About the Author

Hi, Everyone! I'm a USA Today Bestselling Author and I write super-sexy paranormal romance fiction designed to be as much an adventure as a soul-satisfying experience. With every book, I try to give a taste of real life, despite the fact that I'm writing about hunky vampire warriors. You'll come away engrossed in the lives of my vampires as they wage war, as they make love, and as they answer the tough questions of life in terms of purpose, eternity, and how to raise a family! I began my career with Kensington Publishing writing Regency Romance as Valerie King. In 2005, Romantic Times Magazine honored me with a career achievement award in Regency Romance. I've published sixteen paranormal stories to-date, some self-published and some for St. Martin's Press. To find out more about me, please visit my website!

www.carisroane.com

Author of

Guardians of Ascension Series – Warriors of the Blood crave the breh-hedden
Dawn of Ascension Series – Militia Warriors battle to save Second Earth
Blood Rose Series – Only a blood rose can fulfill a mastyr vampire's deepest needs
Blood Rose Tales – Short tales of mastyr vampires who hunger to be satisfied
Men in Chains Series – Vampires struggling to get free of their chains and save the world

Other Titles:

RAPTURE'S EDGE 1 AWAKENING

BLOOD ROSE SERIES BOX SET, featuring Book #1 EMBRACE THE DARK and Book #2 EMBRACE THE MAGIC

EMBRACE THE DARK #1

EMBRACE THE MAGIC #2

EMBRACE THE MYSTERY #3

EMBRACE THE PASSION #4

EMBRACE THE NIGHT #5

BLOOD ROSE TALES BOX SET

TO PURCHASE THE BLOOD ROSE TALES SEPARATELY:

TRAPPED

HUNGER

SEDUCED

THE DARKENING

VAMPIRE COLLECTION (Includes BRINK OF ETERNITY)

WICKED NIGHT/DARK NIGHT (Boxed Set)

CPSIA information can be obtained
at www.ICGtesting.com
Printed in the USA
FSOW02n1104090217
30618FS